FRONTIER
LAWMAN

Also Available in Large Print
by Lee Floren

Renegade Gambler
Smoky River

FRONTIER LAWMAN

LEE FLOREN

G.K. HALL & CO.

Boston, Massachusetts

1981

Library of Congress Cataloging in Publication Data

Floren, Lee.
  Frontier lawman.

  Large print ed.
  1. Large type books.   I. Title.
  [PS3511.L697F7   1981]   813'.52   81-6852
  ISBN 0-8161-3238-0   AACR2

Published in Large Print by arrangement
with Lee Floren.

Set in Compugraphic 18 pt English Times
by Theresa Delehanty

FRONTIER LAWMAN

CHAPTER 1

Bucky O'Neill was in the courthouse that scorching August day in 1881 when the transplanted tough Texas cowboys from the Tonto Basin decided to "tree" the pioneer town of Phoenix in Arizona Territory.

The Texans hit the end of Phoenix's graveled main street with their broncs bucking and their long six-shooters hammering lead into the Arizona blue sky.

Phoenix's natives — mostly of Spanish descent — either ran for their lives or barricaded themselves in their adobe shacks.

Twenty-one-year-old Bucky had been looking up the week's record in the town marshal's office for his newspaper, *The Herald,* when the shooting began; the scream of fleeing citizens was discernible even above the staccato roar of six-shooters.

Marshal Enrique Garfias pushed back his old swivel chair, his lean, dark middle-aged Latin face showing anger. "These danged Texans again," the lawman said shortly. "Last week I ordered them to ride into town without scaring everybody half to death, but I guess they thought I was joking."

Bucky looked up from an Official Record. "What are you going to do, marshal?"

Marshal Garfias got to his feet; he was a very short man just two inches under Bucky's five-nine. "Stop them someway," he said. "That's my job. I assumed it when I pinned on this marshal badge last election."

"Alone?"

"Who's to help me? County won't provide funds for an assistant marshal. And besides who would want to go out and face those tough Texans?"

Bucky nodded, his youthful face serious. Apparently he sought a decision to some problem, for his boyish face was a mirror of conflicting emotions. Finally he ran his hand through his black hair, his gray-blue eyes on the lawman.

"I'll help you, marshal."

Marshal Garfias, the father of six, gave the young newspaper reporter a quick look. "This might lead to gunsmoke. Some of us might not walk off from this, Bucky. We might be toted out of the street on a door."

Bucky said, "I've been in the Territory two years now. From the day I rode in I had a gun on my hip. The dump is filled with cans I've blasted into Kingdom Come with my six-shooter."

"They've told me about your practicing in the town dump." The marshal cocked his head, listening. "They're about three blocks away from where Sunset Street comes into Main. Raise your right hand, Bucky, and repeat, fast, after me, *por favor.*"

Within a minute, Bucky had been sworn in as Marshal Enrique Garfias' deputy marshal. Within another minute, the new deputy marshal was with Marshal Garfias out in the street, awaiting the Texans.

Thus for the first time William Owen O'Neill was a lawman with a star on his vest; it was not destined to be his last time as a badge toter. What were his thoughts as he stood there, knuckles white on the black handle of his holstered Colt .44?

Two years before, he'd ridden into pioneer Phoenix on a burro he'd bought in Santa Fe, Territory of New Mexico, on his long train and burro ride to Arizona.

Because he'd learned the printing trade in his native Virginia, he'd gone to work immediately for *The Herald,* owned by an Arizona pioneer named Charlie McClintock.

From printer he'd graduated to part-time reporter, for McClintock had been ailing somewhat of late.

What if his father, Captain John O'Neill, were to see him now standing in this dusty street ready to stop these mad, gunslinging Texans?

Bucky reckoned his father would have been proud of him, for Captain O'Neill had received five wounds fighting for the Union at Fredericksburg and now was Provost Marshal of Washington, D. C. where Bucky'd been born.

And his gentle mother —

Bucky didn't like to think of his mother

at this moment, for she had a terrible fear and dislike of guns and violence. In fact, he'd had to beg her to allow his father to even buy him a .22 rifle, the first repeating rifle to be sold — a Winchester lever-action repeater.

"Well," Marshal Enrique Garfias said, "here they come. You take the left side of the street, Bucky, and I'll take the right. That way we'll have them penned between us."

Bucky moved to his left, his high-heeled cowboy boots crunching gravel, his heart hammering so hard he later reported he thought it would pound its way out of his ribs.

"You keep your gun in leather if possible," the marshal said. "I don't want you hurt. I'll fire once in the air and try to stop them. Here they come, Bucky!"

Now the loud Texans, horses bucking and rearing, roared down on them, and Marshal Garfias lifted his heavy pistol, blasting a shell close to the head of the lead Texan.

The man lifted his bronc by its reins, his eyes were savage and mean under his wide brimmed hat. "What's here?" he demanded, as his three saddle pals drew rein behind him, smoking pistols in their rope-calloused hands.

"You're under arrest unless you hand your guns over to me and my deputy," the marshal stated.

All of Phoenix watched from curtained windows or from roofs and safe places along the street.

"I don't like Mexicans," the leader said. "I'm a Texan, *sabe?*"

"I know you're Texan," the marshal said, "but this is Arizona. Fun is fun but this is not fun. Either you throw me down your guns or you turn around and leave town, Texan."

The challenge was there — abrupt, deadly, certain. Bucky knew that a Texan without a gun on his hip was the same as a Texan without clothes, and he instinctively tensed, gun half raised from its holster.

For one long second, the four big Texans eyed Marshal Enrique Garfias and Deputy Marshal Bucky O'Neill, and then the big lead Texan snarled, "Clean the street, cowboys!"

The shooting began. . . . Instantly the

graveled street was a bloody arena of violent action.

Guns belched. Horses neighed, reared. Powdersmoke rose chokingly. Dust geysered at Bucky's boots. His gun kicked back against his palm as he shot with deadly accuracy.

His first bullet smashed into the right thigh of the Texans' leader, knocked him sprawling from his saddle, the Texan hollering in pain as he dropped his gun.

Bucky's second bullet hit a Texan's right arm, sending the man's gun spinning. Then, suddenly, the fight was over.

Bucky realized, dimly, that he'd not had time to be afraid, and he also realized he'd not been shot, although how the Texans could have missed him at such close range remained a mystery to him to the day of his death, and Bucky O'Neill died before really reaching his prime.

Three Texans were unhorsed, having been shot into the dust. Their broncs whirled and ran wildly back down-street, stirrups flapping. One horse — a big sorrel — stepped on his loose trailing reins.

The sorrel went tail over tincup, landing flatly on his saddle. Even from that distance, Bucky heard either the cantle or fork — or both — crack loudly under the bronc's lunging weight.

The horse scrambled to his hoofs, trembling with fear. He ran no further but stood still, his lesson learned. The other broncs, wiser than he, ran with heads to one side, thus making their reins trail where there'd be no danger of stepping on them.

Bucky shot a glance at Marshal Garfias, who was unwounded. Bucky dimly remembered the marshal's lead pitching one Texan from saddle. The only Texan remaining in saddle had his hands shoulder high, his gun having been thrown into the dust. He'd had enough of Bucky and Marshal Garfias.

"No more!" the Texan hollered. "I've had enough!"

"More than enough," gritted a wounded Texan.

The town doctor came on the run. He treated the wounded Texans as best he could and had them transported to his big two-story home, which served as the local hospital.

When on their feet again the Texans would go before the local justice-of-the-peace for a hearing. Bucky and Marshal Garfias went into the marshal's office where Bucky dipped a dipper of water from the pail. To his surprise and chagrin, his hand trembled violently.

"After-shock," Marshal Garfias said. "No man is without fear, despite what the dime novels say. A hero is only a man who can conquer and shove back his fear."

"I'm no hero then," Bucky said, handing the dipper to the marshal. "I was really scared out there."

"But you shot true and fast," the marshal reminded him.

"I had to," Bucky said, grinning. "If I hadn't they'd have killed me. Here's your badge, marshal."

"Hope you never have to wear it again," the lawman said. "Here, we fill out a time voucher. The county owes you some money, you know."

Bucky looked at the big wall clock. "Won't be much, marshal. No more than half an hour of county work. I don't believe this is the end of the Texans, though."

Marshal Garfias knew what Bucky meant. The big Hashknife outfit from the Texas Panhandle had driven thousands of heads of cattle into the Tonto Basin area, some fifty miles northeast of pioneer Phoenix.

For days Texas longhorns had spilled over the Mogollon Rim into Tonto Basin, much to the anger of local ranchers, most of these being sheepmen from Utah.

Already there'd been clashes between these sheepmen and the Texans, but nothing serious had as yet transpired. Such happenings were beyond Marshal Garfias' jurisdiction, though, for his authority extended only to the limits of the city of Phoenix, if Phoenix at that time could have been called a city.

Arizona Rangers had the unhappy chore of keeping peace in Tonto Basin and as one ranger said, "When they named it Tonto Basin they named it correctly, because Tonto means Fool in Spanish, and sometimes I think there's not a sensible person living in the entire Basin."

Marshal Garfias called a town meeting

that night at the court house steps. He publicly thanked Bucky for siding with him against the Texans and expressed the belief that when word got to the Texans' cow camp that one Texan was in Phoenix's jail and three others in the makeshift hospital the other Texans would ride in a tough body into Phoenix to "tree the town and take the town apart."

Bucky was commissioned to organize a Vigilance Committee among the local citizens.

Marshal Garfias stressed that Bucky met many, many people in his rounds as a newspaper reporter and therefore was in a good position to do such organizing, and next evening Bucky had twenty men out in military formation on the courthouse lawn, each man equipped with a rifle and a side-arm.

Word of the rough gunfight had quickly spread through the sparsely settled Territory and the name of *Bucky O'Neill* suddenly took on a greater importance. Tough Arizonians decided this newspaper reporter wasn't a man to be trifled with.

Bucky tried desperately to remember all the military commands his Civil War veteran father had taught him, but his memory failed. Nevertheless, he found a military manual among some court house books; this aided him and the second night of drill found his small *army* moving more rapidly and competently through its paces.

Now let us take a clearer look at this five-foot-nine young man of twenty-one summers whom Arizonians to this day call Bucky O'Neill and whom Arizonians to this day — almost a century later — point to with pride.

Let us return to the day of his birth in Virginia.

CHAPTER 2

Crouched in the thick Virginia brush, the big quail waited until the boy had walked past and then, when the youthful hunter's back was toward him, he boomed out of his hiding place, wings roaring.

Hurriedly, thirteen-year-old Bucky O'Neill whirled, rifle automatically rising to his shoulder. Sighting desperately, he fired two times as rapidly as he could work the lever of his rifle — but the quail, with a saucy flirt of his tail, soared out of sight into a hollow, unhurt.

Frowning, Bucky lowered his rifle. He should have hit that quail . . . but he hadn't and he couldn't blame it on his rifle, either.

His rifle was a brand new Winchester lever-action repeater that had just been released on the market in this year of 1873

— the first repeating .22 caliber ever made in the United States.

It shot both .22 shorts and .22 long rifle cartridges. His father, Captain John O'Neill, had bought it for his youngest boy just yesterday, and Bucky was very, very proud of it.

No, it was not the rifle's fault; it was his. Some Arizona pioneer he'd make! A good rifleman would have sent that flying quail tumbling to earth, a mass of feathers!

Unless he learned to shoot better, he'd starve trying to live off the land out in Arizona Territory. For some day — when grown — he was heading west to Arizona.

He was sure of that. After his schooling was finished off west he would go . . . with his rifle under his arm!

He now wished he had a bird dog, for a pointer would show him where quail were hidden; but he owned no dog and that was that.

He would also have to watch his supply of cartridges for .22 shells were expensive, selling at four cents a box of fifty long-rifles. A quail hunter needed long-rifle cartridges for sometimes quail would perch on rail fences quite a distance away — and a short shell couldn't reach them.

Suddenly, he froze in his tracks.

Forty yards away was a rickety old rail fence. A big quail had just hopped out of the tall grass and was now perched on the fence's bottom rail, saucy and inviting.

The quail's head jerked this way and that as he nervously searched for enemies. Although he must have seen Bucky he apparently didn't think the boy dangerous for he made no move to fly away.

Bucky dropped quickly to his knees, rifle rising to his shoulder. Muscles trembling, he tried to center the rifle's sights on the quail, but his hands shook dreadfully, the rifle's barrel fairly dancing.

Angry desperation tore through him. He had to fire — and fire soon — or the quail would either fly away or drop back into the grass and be lost.

He gritted his teeth. He momentarily closed his eyes and when he opened them his vision was more sure. Finally, by sheer physical effort of mind over matter he got the front sight in the notch of the rear . . . and pulled the trigger!

There was no smokeless powder in cartridges in those days and smoke rose and hid the quail. Bucky leaped to his feet. He stared at the fence's bottom rail. The quail was gone!

He had missed! While powdersmoke had hidden the quail the quail had dropped back into the high grass. Now he would be running quickly through the tall foliage, short legs working madly, as he fled to safety.

Breathing heavily, Bucky's blue eyes carefully searched the horizon, but they saw no quail flying away. Bucky walked sadly toward the fence, silently bewailing his ill fortune and inadequate shooting ability.

He stopped suddenly and stared at the grass under the fence, his heart pounding wildly.

There lay the quail, feathers scattered around him!

"I got him!" Bucky screamed. "I got him!"

Quickly he scooped up the bloody quail and did a little Indian dance of joy, the kind he'd read about the Arizona Apaches dancing after a successful war-raid.

How proud Dad would be! And now Mom would have a quail to cook for supper! Then, he stared soberly at the quail's closed eyes and limp neck.

He felt sorry for the beautiful bird and, at the same time, he felt proud of himself. Then the thought came that a family as big as Dad's and Mom's — five, in all — could not feed satisfactorily on one single quail. He'd have to shoot more!

He crammed the quail into his packsack and continued tramping the Virginia woods, the sweet perfume of ivy and growing plants loving his boyish nostrils. He saw two more coveys of quail but they were wild and soared away before he could reach rifle range.

With a slight start, he noticed that the sun had already set. Dusk was creeping through the woods. It was time he started for home.

When he arrived home his father was trimming the roses in the spacious yard of the big home. Captain O'Neill looked up and smiled. "Any luck, son?"

"One, Dad."

"Good."

His father carefully examined the quail

and Bucky, watching his father's rugged face, saw his dad smile softly, and Bucky's heart leaped with joy.

"Mother's in the kitchen preparing supper. Let's show it to her, huh?"

Although Bucky's mother said, "Ugh," she hugged her youngest son's small shoulders, and Bucky understood.

His mother had a terrible fear of guns for his father had been wounded many times in the Civil War, having received five wounds in the battle of Fredericksburg.

Captain O'Neill now walked with the aid of a cane. He had organized Company K, 116th Pennsylvania Volunteers, and he was now provost marshal of the military police in Washington, D. C.

Because of his mother's dislike of guns Bucky had had to argue long and diligently before she'd consented to allowing Bucky to have his new .22 rifle. Finally, after much persuasion on the part of Bucky, she allowed his father to buy him the gun.

Bucky and his father had made a bargain: his father would buy the rifle but it was up to Bucky to make enough money to keep himself in cartridges.

Now Bucky solemnly said, "I'm not a good shot, though. I missed one easy shot and where I'm going when I get big a man has to be a dead shot because he has to live off the country — wild turkeys and deer and antelope and wild game like that."

He saw his father suppress a slight smile. "And where is this mystic country located that you are going to, Mister Bucky, when you are a man?"

"Arizona Territory, Dad."

"And why Arizona instead of, say, Montana or Idaho or Maine or Vermont?"

Bucky shook his head. "I just can't tell you, Dad, because I don't know just why for sure myself, but to Arizona I'm going."

His father tapped him lightly with his cane. "Then if your mind is made up to go to Arizona, someday you'll go there, son. Now get something to eat and go upstairs and do your studies and be in bed by eight — and eight sharp, too."

"Ah, Dad. . . ."

"Hurry along, son."

Later that evening Bucky slipped downstairs for a drink of water. His parents were talking in the living room and he shamelessly eavesdropped — a small pajama-clad figure crouched behind the door.

"That William Owen," his mother sighed.

Bucky winced. William Owen were his given names and he detested them with all the vehemence a small boy can muster.

When he got to Arizona he'd never let anybody know that his name was William Owen O'Neill. He would be always called Bucky. Dad had called him Bucky ever since he could remember. He never did know where Dad had got the idea of calling him Bucky.

"What about Bucky?" his father asked.

"He's reading all the time. The only time he lays down a book is when he tramps through the woods and the last year he's read about every book published on Arizona, I really do believe."

"That doesn't sound too bad to me, Mama."

"He's studied every map he can find on Arizona. He knows every river and stream by heart and where it's located in Arizona.''

"That shouldn't be hard. Arizona hasn't much water, you know, except a bit in the northern part, but it's most all desert.''

"Where'd you learn so much about Arizona?''

Captain John O'Neill smiled. "By reading, the same as Bucky. But you sound a little worried, darling.''

"I am, Dad. I'm afraid that when he gets a little bigger he might run away to Arizona, for so many young boys are going West in these troubled times.''

Captain John nodded understandingly.

"And I do hope he gets a good education before he leaves for if Bucky makes up his mind to leave, Bucky will leave. When he's determined to do something, do it Bucky does!''

Bucky's father considered this. "We'll do our best to keep him in school until he gets his college degree,'' he said slowly, "but all young birds have to fly away from the home nest sometime, you know.''

"Yes, I know that, but. . . .''

"If I weren't so danged crippled — and a few years younger — Bucky might have his father along for company, you know."

"Oh, go on now!"

Bucky crept upstairs and back to bed, where he lay in the dark mulling over what he'd heard.

Sometimes school was a chore and a bore but other times it got real interesting, especially when the class studied the Western states and territories. He sighed deeply and instantly fell asleep.

He learned the printing trade in high school, for he reasoned that a knowledge of printing might come in handy in pioneer Arizona.

He also became efficient in shorthand by studying it in college and high school. He was only nineteen when he got a law degree from National University.

He was immediately licensed to practice law in Washington, D. C., the youngest barrister admitted to the bar in Washington to that date.

His mother sighed, feeling easier now. He might settle down close to home and practice law.

But the call of the open spaces of the

great far West still echoed in his ears, although buffalo hunting on the Great Plains was practically a thing of the past in this year of 1879, for the buffalo had been ruthlessly and needlessly slaughtered.

Three years ago General George A. Custer and his entire command of the Seventh Cavalry had been annihilated on the Little Big Horn River in the Territory of Montana.

The combined forces of the Sioux and Cheyenne had wiped out Custer's complete regiment in one of the greatest victories the redman had ever attained over the palefaces. After Custer had fallen General Nelson Appleton Miles had moved in on the Plains with his troops and now all Indian trouble was over except for a few scattered Apache raids in the twin territories of New Mexico and Arizona.

Virginia and the East were growing too crowded to suit Bucky. This area held no new adventures. He could see himself growing old and gray practicing law and working out of stuffy offices and this vision of his future soured his youthful stomach.

Also Spring rode the balmy air, firing his blood. He stood it until the middle of June and then he said, "Mother and Dad, I can't help it. I don't like this country. I'm going West."

His father said, "We've been sort of expecting this from you, Bucky. It's your life to live, not ours — and you only have one time to go around the clock, you know."

"That's the way I look at it, Dad."

"You've finished your education. Our blessings go with you, son."

His mother smiled through tears. "Write us often from Arizona, son," she said.

Bucky rode the rails to Albuquerque, New Mexico Territory, and there he bought a burro which he rode overland southwest to the small village of Phoenix, Arizona, set on the desert beside the Gila River, which for most of the year was dry, he later learned.

He single-footed his burro into Phoenix one scorching hot day while the town had its siesta, for Phoenix had more inhabitants of Mexican descent than of Anglo-Saxon and these Mexicans kept to the old siesta habit of their native land, all industry and work being stopped each afternoon from two until four.

Despite the blistering heat, happiness was in nineteen-year-old Bucky O'Neill's heart. Arizona had proved to be all he'd dreamed about . . . and more.

North were dim heat-drenched mountains. The desert stretched south, west and east — an endless sweep of gray smoketrees and clumps of green spiny mesquite.

Now all he needed was a job, and one was immediately forthcoming. Heavy-set, middle-aged Charles McClintock, owner of the town's only newspaper, the *Phoenix Herald,* needed a man who could set type and write news stories.

Bucky was employed in the *Herald's* print shop an hour after riding into Phoenix. For two years now he had written news stories, sold advertising space, and set type for the *Herald*, not to mention keeping the books, also.

He'd never used his law degree but he'd used his gun. And now Phoenix sat back and waited uneasily for the Texans to come.

"Those Texans will never allow a

Hashknife rider to stay in jail," said a former Texan, now a resident of Phoenix.

Bucky shrugged. "They'll have to pull the jail down to get him out, Rube."

"They'll do just that, Bucky. After they've killed a few people, of course."

"We can only wait and see, Rube."

CHAPTER 3

The Texans hit Phoenix the Saturday following the gunfight which established young Bucky O'Neill as a top-notch gunslinger.

Marshal Garfias and Bucky had stationed guards night and day along the trails leading into the pioneer town. They'd also put men on high buttes surrounding Phoenix. From this lofty vantage the men could see the country for miles around.

All guards were experienced desert men with good eyesight. Born and bred on the range, they could tell a cow from a horse — or vice versa — as soon as they saw an animal, no matter how distant the animal was.

Rube guarded the Tonto Basin Trail. At ten after nine Saturday night the lanky

Arizonian rode madly into town, whipping his hard-running horse down the hind legs for more speed.

He pulled his horse to a dust-rising, skidding stop in front of the court house. He threw down his reins, lifted a leg over his saddle's horn and left his Parker saddle on the dead run, landing with boot heels digging.

"Marshal Garfias — Bucky —"

"Yes, Rube, what is it?" Marshal Garfias demanded.

"They're comin', marshal. The Texans — they're comin' — Tonto Basin road, men!"

Rube reported he'd counted twenty-two Texans, and his field glasses had shown them heavily armed with pistols strapped to hips and rifles jammed butt-up into leather saddle-boots.

Marshal Garfias and Bucky exchanged glances. "How far away were they, Rube?" Bucky asked.

"I was on Rock Mesa. That's a good four miles from here. They was about a mile beyond me when they rode up out of Killigan Canyon, big as life and twice as tough!"

Bucky rubbed his jaw. "Don't look natural for them to be coming in the Tonto Basin Trail, right where we'd be looking for them, marshal."

"I was thinking the same," Marshal Garfias said. "They could branch north on Lost Willow Trail, though, and then swing west and come into town from the trail to Wickenburg."

"Or they might leave their cayuses on the edge of town and split up and come in in pairs or in threes or fours, marshal," Bucky reminded.

"That's possible and probable. If they do take Lost Willow Trail, we should be getting a report real soon from Mack, 'cause he's watching northwest along Lost Willow."

"Here he comes now," Rube said.

Bucky's vigilantes were entering the court house by side and rear doors, not daring to come in the front for fear that the Texans would have a spy in Phoenix who might report back to the Texans that Bucky had organized vigilantes, for Bucky and his men had done their best to keep their existence a secret. Bucky could only hope they'd done just that.

Now some thirty-odd men were in Marshal Garfias' quarters, some of them veterans of the Civil War and others men who'd fought the Indian Wars on the frontier — tough, grizzled men who sought peace, their days of devilry and hell-raising behind.

Mack came in on the run. "They took Lost Willow Trail from Tonto Basin road, men. They rode down along Green Creek and it looks like they're going to split up there and infiltrate the town on foot."

Bucky nodded. "Then they'll meet somewhere in town and band up and start the fireworks, huh? Joe should have a report on this. Where is he, I wonder?"

Joe was stationed on the west edge of town in the high brush. "Here he comes now on the dead run," a vigilante member said.

"Wonder where his cayuse is?" another asked.

Joe reported his horse had stumbled over a mesquite and had injured his off front leg. He also reported that the Texans had ridden into a grove of cottonwood trees along a creek and hadn't ridden out.

"I got up high on Crystal Butte where I

could look down. They aim to come into town on foot, I guess — sneak in under cover of night.''

''Too much moon for that,'' Bucky said. ''Rube here says the moonlight is so bright he could see that each one was armed with a side-arm and a rifle on his saddle.''

''Well, I *reckoned* each was so armed,'' Rube hurriedly said.

''They leave a man with their horses?'' Bucky asked.

''Two men, looked to me.''

Bucky looked at Marshal Garfias. ''Odd that a cowboy'd want to fight on foot but I can see their point of view. They're afraid that if they rode in in a group we might be ready for them and cut them to pieces while they were on horses, like what happened to those other four the other day.''

The marshal nodded. ''I'll send a man or so out to get their horses from that guard. Then if they do break through us and made a dash back for their broncs they'll be afoot for good because no horses will be waiting for them in that grove.''

"Good idea," Bucky said.

"What'd you intend to do with your vigilantes?" the lawman asked.

Bucky grinned. "Beat the Texans at their own game. I'm going to have each vigilante trail a Texan in and see to it that that particular Texan doesn't reach the rendezvous the Texans have picked here in town."

Marshal Garfias chuckled despite the gravity of the situation. "Knock each one over the coconut, huh? And then what?"

"Fill the jail," Bucky said grimly. "We can't put any more in Doc's hospital. It's full now."

"We still got the graveyard with a few hundred empty lots," a grizzled merchant said. "I got a wife and three cute little girls and no wild killers gonna touch a hair on their heads!"

"Same goes for me," another married man said positively.

Bucky had a black moment. He'd tried to pick all single men for this dangerous job but there hadn't been enough of such in Phoenix to make a vigilante committee, so he'd had to include married men. He'd then tried to organize married men without children but that had been an impossibility.

"Men, be careful," he said. "I want you all to come back safe and sound to your families."

"We'd best make tracks. Here comes Red," the marshal said.

Red reported that the Texans had come out of the trees on foot and had spread out and plainly were going to infiltrate Phoenix under cover of night and through this way band again and, as Red said, "tree the danged whole town!"

Hurriedly, Bucky assigned his vigilantes to alleys and streets, the men hurriedly leaving in grim silence, and finally only he and the marshal were in the courthouse.

"I'll patrol the streets like nothing's happened," Marshal Garfias said. "That way, if they have a spy in town he'll see me out in the street and think I'm completely in the dark."

"I don't think the spy will be a he," Bucky said. "I think it'll be a she and one of the girls — or even Madame Jones herself — that will be on the lookout, if anybody is."

"You could be right," the marshal said.

"Those Texans spend a lot of money on Madame Jones and her girls. Where you going to be, Bucky?"

Bucky smiled. "Rube said Luke Savage heads those Texans and that's right, because he's their range boss. I hope Rube's right. And I hope I'm the one that runs into Mr. Savage."

"He's tough, Bucky."

"He's also good story material," Bucky said. "I can see the headlines of the extra McClintock and I will put out if this thing comes off. Herald *reporter captures outlaw leader,* or some such thing."

"Hope it isn't *Texan ramrod slays* Herald *reporter.*" The marshal made it sound like a joke, which it definitely was not.

Bucky slapped his friend on the back. "Don't get pessimistic in your old age, Enrique."

He and the marshal spoke in Spanish, a tongue they used whenever alone. Bucky had asked the marshal to talk to him in Spanish, for he desperately wanted to learn that language.

Here in Phoenix more conversations were carried on in Spanish than in English and unless a person knew Spanish he'd miss many things. A newspaper reporter, Bucky knew, had to keep his ears open . . . and what was more important he had to understand what his ears heard.

Bucky slipped into the moonlight, aware of his heavy Colts tied low on his hips, the buckskin tiedown thong rubbing against the inside of his muscular thigh.

For one moment, he glanced up at the round Arizona moon. That same moon lighted his old Virginia home. How many years had passed since he'd left his father and mother and brothers and sisters behind?

Only two, of course. . . . Two short, busy years in this land he'd grown to love — a land that seemed more to be his than had even the land of his birth, Virginia.

He shoved such thoughts from his mind. Ahead lay danger and possibly deadly gunsmoke. He remembered eight years back to his first rifle, the .22 repeater his father had bought him.

But he was hunting more than quail here in Arizona. Where would the Texans hold their rendezvous? Phoenix citizens had a definitely outlined saloon and roughneck district three blocks long and slightly separated from the respectable residential section.

Madame Jones' saloon and tenderloin emporium, the biggest building in the redlight district, was the usual hangout for the Hashknife Texans, and because it was their favorite hangout and everybody would expect them to meet there, Bucky figured they'd not meet there.

He'd had hard words with Luke Savage, Hashknife ramrod, about two months ago when Savage had come into the *Herald* office objecting to something Bucky had written about the roughness of Hashknife men when in town.

Bucky had pointed out that he'd written only the truth, for hadn't a Hashknife almost bucked a horse over a three-year-old boy toddling across Main Street? Luke Savage had stated that it was the job of a mother to keep track of her children and not allow them in the street where a cowboy who had a horse that wanted to buck was in danger of riding the child down.

Bucky had pointed out that the Hashknife cowboy in question hadn't been

36

riding a bronc that *wanted* to buck; the cowboy had deliberately *made* his horse buck by kicking him high in the flanks with his wicked Mexican spurs.

The argument had got rather warm — so warm that big Charlie McClintock had pushed his bulk between the two men, threatening to call Marshal Garfias if Luke Savage didn't leave the *Herald*'s premises.

Savage had invited Bucky out in the alley to finish the argument with fists or with guns but Bucky, realizing the argument was foolish to begin with, politely declined. Savage had called him "yellow."

Bucky then offered to go with Savage into the alley but Marshal Garfias, having seen Savage enter the *Herald*'s office from the court house window, suddenly came in and told Savage to mind his own business.

"This ain't finished yet, pen-pusher," Luke Savage had snarled at Bucky upon leaving.

Bucky figured tonight was as good a time as any to finish his trouble with Luke Savage, for he knew that sooner or later it had to be brought to a culmination. He'd heard that word had got around Phoenix that he was indeed "yellow" for not going into the alley with Luke Savage when the Hashknife ramrod had first challenged him.

Of course, the shootout with the Texans had removed all doubts about his courage, but he still wanted to collect Luke Savage tonight just to show various people in town that he was man enough to trim Savage's "wick," as the pioneer saying went.

But Bucky didn't get to capture or gunfight Luke Savage. This dubious task fell upon the townsman, Rube, who ran into Savage in the alley. Soon both Rube and Savage had roaring guns. Savage was killed in the battle and Rube suffered a broken leg that made him limp the rest of his life.

Bucky ran into another Hashknife rider; he didn't know the man. He saw him slyly entering an alley. He ran ahead and got ahead of the man and stepped out when the man got close enough.

"Going somewhere, Hashknife?" Bucky had asked.

"None of your danged business,

scissorbill. Ain't you the pen-pusher from the stinkin' newspaper?"

"I'm O'Neill," Bucky assured. "And the *Herald* don't stink. Where's your horse?"

"I'm on foot tonight."

"That's odd," Bucky said. "I've heard that no one in Texas ever walks, that they ride a horse from the barn even though the barn's only a few feet away."

Both men were down in a crouch flinging words at each other. Moonlight washed across the Hashknife man's wide, florid face, for his big Amarillo broadbrim was pushed back over his sandy-colored hair.

Bucky noticed the cowboy's eyes were on his right shoulder. He'd heard that experienced gunmen didn't watch a man's eyes or his gun; they kept their gaze riveted on their opponent's shoulder — the right shoulder for a right-handed gunman, the left for a left-handed.

For when a man draws a short-gun from a holster, the tip of his shoulder is the first part of his body that moves as he makes his draw. Bucky realized he faced an experienced gunman.

He was momentarily angry with himself. He hadn't needed to come out in front of this gunman. He could have played it safe and sure and come in silently behind the gunman and slugged him cold with the barrel of his Colts Peacemaker.

He'd thought of that, too, before stepping into this alley and challenging this cowboy but, somehow, that hadn't seemed what his father would have called "cricket."

He knew that Hashknife had many, many fast gunslingers on its Arizona payroll. Hashknife had expected trouble when it had trailed in fifty thousand head of cattle onto grass already slightly over-grazed by sheep, the cowman's deadly enemy.

"I'll tell you why you're afoot." Bucky's voice sounded cramped and distant even in his own ears. "You Texans hid your broncs in the trees west of town. You aim to sneak into town and meet and then present a solid front and take the town over."

"You — had spies — out?"

"We sure did. And right now a vigilante is following each of the Hashknife men, even Luke Savage."

"Luke'll kill you for this. He missed killing you the other day because that big fat editor of yours —"

Savage distant gunfire stopped the man short. Bucky realized one of the vigilantes — or Marshal Garfias — had crossed guns with a Hashknife man. He silently prayed momentarily that the Phoenix man had come out on top.

Bucky said, "Put your hands up, mister. You can't tree this town, Texan. Why not raise your hands and give up and go to jail and get it over with?"

"You ain't takin' me to jail, pen-pusher!"

Bucky was getting rather weary of being called pen-pusher, but didn't mention that. Such trivialities had no place in a situation this serious. Somewhere a cricket made a loud creaking sound. This rasped against Bucky's nerves.

He had to get the best of this man, but how? He tried a trick as old as gunfighting. "Right now there's a man behind you with a gun, cowboy, so why not raise your hands?"

The man laughed hoarsely. "That's so

old it's got a beard. I tell you, O'Neill, I — What the heck was that?"

Bucky had heard boots scrape somewhere behind the gunman, also. The gunman suddenly turned his side to Bucky so he could cover Bucky and look back at the same time . . . and during that split second Bucky O'Neill saw his chance.

He flung his muscular body forward like a cougar leaping from a crag onto an unsuspecting deer. He hit the man around the shoulders with stunning force, a prayer in his throat that he manage to grab the man's gun while it rose from holster, for one glimpse as he flew forward told him the Hashknife man was making his draw.

The man went down, screaming something. Another fear now hit Bucky: what if the approaching man were Hashknife and not one of his vigilantes? If so, he was doomed!

He decided he'd have to trust to luck and hope the man was a vigilante. He now had the man's gun by the barrel, the man on the ground under him. Savagely, they fought momentarily for the pistol, but Bucky was on top and leverage was in his favor.

He'd also driven a thumb between hammer and frame. The man pulled the trigger; the hammer fell. To his untimely death he bore the scar of that gun hammer on the curvature of his thumb.

Nauseating pain surged through his arm. When he did get the gun, it hung from his thumb; desperately, he got it loose, the other man still trying to reach for his gun.

But Bucky now had complete control of the Texan's gun. Twice the barrel came down, socking bone and hair. The man ceased struggling. Hurriedly, the borrowed gun in hand, Bucky leaped to his feet, the pistol covering the area in the moonlight from whence had come what had sounded like the sound of cowboy boots.

"Who's there?"

No answer. Bucky moved forward, knees wooden. He breathed deeply, still not believing he'd evade a gunfight . . . and possible bloody death here in this garbage-can lined alley.

"Who's there?" he repeated, knees steadier now.

Again, no answer. He stood tense in the moonlight, the gun still in hand, his blue eyes probing shadows . . . and finding nothing out of place. He frowned, for he'd been sure boots had come in behind the now-sleeping gunman.

"Who's —"

He got no further. He heard a dog growl in a shed. He went to the small building. Moonlight came in through a window. The door was open. A mother dog lay with four puppies.

She growled at him, eyes glinting in the moonlight streaming through the door. He noticed she and her pups were gnawing on a big bone that still had some red meat on it.

He remembered a butcher shop was located at the end of the alley. Evidently the dog had somehow got hold of the big bone there. What he'd thought had been boots had evidently been the sound made by the bitch dragging the big bone.

Bucky suddenly realized he was sweating. Well, the night was warm; all summer nights were hot in Phoenix. He returned to his victim who still slept soundly, mouth in the dust.

Bucky got the limp form over his shoulder. He toted the unconscious man onto Main Street, where he met some of his vigilantes herding disgusted cowboys, some very bloody, ahead of them as they headed for the jail in the court house.

"Who was doing the shooting?" he asked Joe.

Joe told him that Rube had crossed guns with Luke Savage. "He killed Savage with two shots, his first just disabling the ramrod. Savage got in one shot. It broke Rube's right leg. Rube's in the doctor's office now."

"Anybody else of ours hurt?"

"Not that I know of, but it isn't all over yet. We haven't got all these sonsofguns yet, you know. There goes some more shooting."

The shooting turned out to have been Marshal Garfias shooting it out with two Hashknife men in front of Madame Jones' resort, the marshal being safely ensconced behind a rock wall.

He shot one Hashknife man through the right shoulder, putting him out of commission with one shot, the other man then lost his nerve and started to run. The marshal put three shots at this man's boots, a lucky bullet knocking a high heel off, sending the man stumbling and falling on his face.

Marshal Garfias had then leaped on the man and slugged him cold. Soon all Hashknife men except two were rounded up, these two escaping and running for their horses, where they were later captured — making a clean sweep of Hashknife.

Luke Savage was carried to the morgue — a small building used for such a purpose — and Rube was put to bed with his leg in a fracture box. Bucky, Garfias and the vigilance committee — including Charles McClintock — then all repaired to the Horseshoe, where Marshal Garfias went the price of beers.

"County'll pay for it in the end," the genial marshal said. "I'll bill it the first of the month. Bucky, I sort of got a hunch Hashknife won't bother Phoenix any more with Savage dead and the others beat up and wounded and going before the j.p. where we've already agreed to fine each man at least two hundred bucks."

"And if a man can't pay his fine?" Bucky asked.

"One hundred days on the country road

gang making little rocks out of big ones and twenty extra days to pay costs of the court.''

"That should hold them," Bucky said.

Marshal Garfias lowered his voice. "Bucky, I can get the county commissioners to sign you on as my deputy. I don't know what McClintock pays you on the *Herald,* but I'll see your salary as my deputy will be ten dollars a month higher."

Bucky shook his head. "Not this time, Enrique. I got a little more of Arizona I want to see."

"Arizona's made up of two things, Bucky. What don't bite you sticks you."

Bucky lifted his beer. "Rattlesnakes and mesquite thorns," he said. "No, I believe I'll go down Tombstone way for a while and look around. They tell me that silver-mining town is really booming."

Tombstone was about two hundred miles southeast, mostly south. Bucky had met John Clum, owner and publisher of the Tombstone *Epitaph,* a few weeks ago when Clum had happened through Phoenix, and he'd liked the quiet hard-working editor at once. Apparently Clum liked him also.

Clum had told him that any time he, Bucky, came to Tombstone there'd be a job for him. Bucky now suddenly decided to take Clum up on the offer, for he'd been in Phoenix two years — and there was still much of his newly-adopted territory he'd not seen.

Charlie McClintock said, "You get your story, Bucky?"

Bucky grinned. He rather hated to leave Charlie but he'd broken in an apprentice the last year that would fill his shoes both in makeup and editorial on the *Herald.*

"I sure did, boss," Bucky said.

CHAPTER 4

To reach Tombstone, Bucky had to go through Tucson, then a sleepy adobe town of Mexicans or people of Mexican descent. While there he got into trouble or, rather, trouble came searching for him.

He'd stabled his sorrel in the local livery-barn and was heading for the Concho cafe for supper, enjoying the cool of the evening, for Tucson was at a much higher altitude than Phoenix and even on the hottest day the evenings were rather cool, especially when compared with Phoenix's hot nights.

Suddenly, he heard a man cursing behind him. He stopped and turned. A big, burly redheaded man of about thirty had come out of a *cantina*. Even as Bucky watched, the man grabbed the wrist of a passing girl and tried to drag her into the saloon.

The girl, of course, resisted, telling the man in no uncertain terms to let go of her arm. The man grinned and tried to put his arm around her but she escaped. She was a small Mexican girl of about twenty, Bucky judged — and strikingly beautiful in a dark-eyed Latin way.

Bucky immediately noticed that her dress was tub-faded from many washings. This instantly told him she was not a saloon girl for such girls always wore fine clothes. The girl looked like she was of a poor family.

"Mister, please help me," she cried to Bucky.

Bucky realized he was the only man — outside of the bully — on the street. Within a moment, the big redhead would drag the protesting girl into the saloon. Bucky turned and went to the man.

"Why don't you leave the girl be?" he said peacefully. "She apparently isn't the kind you want, mister."

"Who the hell are you to interfere with Red Hopkins, buster?"

Bucky spoke to the girl. "Do you know this man?"

The girl answered in Spanish. "He's a bum who came in a few days ago, *senor*. I've seen him around. I don't know his name. And I don't care to know it, either!"

"Talk a real langwidge," Red Hopkins said shortly. "And go your way, buster, or I'll take you apart to see what makes you tick!"

"That'd be interesting," Bucky said. "Let the girl go, Hopkins. She doesn't want anything to do with you."

"She will after she gets to know me better."

Bucky quickly noticed that saloon hangers-on had come out of *cantinas,* most of them Latins. They regarded him with narrowed, tough eyes. He saw quite a few knifes stuck in belts and sashes before he jerked his eyes back to Red Hopkins and the girl who was trying to get her head around so she could bite Hopkins' hand, an impossible feat.

Bucky was no fool. Red Hopkins was not a Latin but still, he might have friends in this gun-toting, knife-carrying gang that was rapidly gathering. He realized he'd have to act fast or leave the girl to her fate, and this latter appealed less to him than did the former.

Suddenly the girl began to weep, and Bucky knew for sure, then, he had to do something — so William Owen O'Neill went into roaring, fast action.

He stepped in quickly. The heel of his right hand hammered down, catching Hopkins' wrist with terrific force. Bucky had learned this maneuver from one of the toughest men who ever walked the earth, an Arizona ranger captain.

Hopkins yelped in pain. Bucky's blow tore his hand from the girl's arm. The lovely girl scurried to one side, rubbing her arm where the bully's big hands had made it blue.

"Mister, please," she called to Bucky. "Don't get in a fight — for me, *senor!*"

Bucky grinned as he moved ahead, shoulders down in a fighter's crouch, thinking that the girl should have thought of that before — and then Red Hopkins was on him, huge fists working like driving steam-pistons.

They owned a piston's brutal force, too. Bucky O'Neill learned that immediately, for he went under Hopkins' right but the bully's left smashed Bucky hard on the head.

Bucky's Stetson went one direction and had not Bucky O'Neill been in tiptop physical condition he'd undoubtedly have gone the other, but long hours in the saddle had toughened him enough to ride out Red Hopkins' terrible blow.

He had to back-pedal until his head cleared. He heard the crowd yell something, and he guessed it was for Hopkins, for such hangers-on always rooted for the most despicable.

"Get him, Hopkins!"

"Kill the man, Red!"

"Five to one on Red! Six to one on Red! Any takers, men?"

Fists pounding. Hopkins rushed Bucky, for the bully knew he had hurt Bucky. But he underestimated Bucky's ability to recover — and he didn't know that Bucky had helped Marshal Garfias quell Phoenix barroom brawls.

Suddenly, to Hopkins' surprise, Bucky seeemed to come to life. His right smashed into Hopkins' solar plexus.

Bucky guessed that Hopkins outweighed him by at least twenty pounds. He was also sure that Hopkins drank too much, judging from his pot belly — and in this pot belly Bucky O'Neill poured lefts and rights.

Hopkins doubled in pain, gasping for breath. Bucky had the bully in the position he wanted him. He quickly stepped behind Hopkins, grabbed Hopkins by each ear, put his right knee into Hopkins' back . . . and he flipped Hopkins, despite Hopkins' weight, over his shoulder.

The Arizona ranger had taught Bucky that maneuver, also. Hopkins thudded to the ground on his back as Bucky whirled. The bully hit the ground so hard he knocked the wind from himself.

It was all over before the *cantina* hangers-on really realized what had happened. One moment Red Hopkins had been on the point of grinding this smaller stranger to mincemeat; the next moment, Hopkins was sailing through the air so fast he seemed a tanglement of arms and legs, not a human.

Now Red Hopkins lay holding the small of his back, groaning and gasping for air. Bucky couldn't help but grin.

"You're an amateur," he told the bully. "Don't ever take on a professional. He'll kill you."

Hopkins' reply was a groaning curse. Bucky looked at the hangers-on. They drew back slightly, plainly wanting nothing to do with him. He then looked for the girl.

She was not around. He couldn't see her going up street or down street. That's gratitude for you, he thought, picking up his Stetson and creasing it again. He looked back from the corner. Two men were helping Red Hopkins hobble into a saloon.

Hopkins was bent almost double. He had the appearance of looking for something on the ground. Bucky went into the Concho where he ate.

He spent the night sleeping in the livery-barn in the haymow above his horse. The bunk cost him ten cents and he had to agree not to smoke, but inasmuch as he didn't smoke, the livery-barn hostler had nothing to worry about.

Next morning the town marshal looked him up and told him that Red Hopkins had left Tucson early that morning.

"Red really got itchy boots when

somebody told him that you helped clean the Hashknife Texans out of Phoenix, and your name was Bucky O'Neill. They tell Red rightly?"

"I'm Bucky O'Neill."

"I've got a job for you, Mr. O'Neill, if you want it. Deputy marshal, siding me."

"No, thanks," Bucky said. "I'm heading for Tombstone."

"Oh, goin' ramrod the law down there, huh?"

"Hardly," Bucky said. "They've got Johnny Behan and the Earps there, I understand. I don't think they need me. I'm going down and work on John Clum's newspaper, if he's got a job for me."

"Oh, writer, huh?"

"Even poetry and short stories," Bucky said, pulling on his boots, "although I've never sold a short story and have had to give my poetry away. Be pleased if you had breakfast with me, marshal."

"No, thanks. Ol' woman filled me with hotcakes and eggs just about a hour ago. I wish you luck, O'Neill."

"Same to you, marshal."

"Tombstone's a tough one, Mr. O'Neill, so walk light, sir."

"I'll do that, marshal."

Tucson's marshal had made no overstatement when he'd said Tombstone was tough. Tombstone was more than tough — it was wild and woolly, as the saying went.

Saloons had no keys. They never locked up so they needed no keys. Gunfights were ordinary occurrences.

Burly silver miners brushed shoulders with gamblers, pimps, gunfighters, tinhorns, gambling hall girls . . . or what have you. Tombstone's mines poured millions into the shack-made city sitting high on the mountain ridge with the endless desert stretching north, east and south, the mountains behind the town.

John Clum warmly shook his hand. "Certainly I remember you. Bucky O'Neill, formerly of Virginia, now apparently one of Arizona Territory's first water gunfighters."

"What do you mean by that?"

"That run-in with the Hashknife outfit. You and that marshal shooting it out with four Texans on the street. News like that gets around fast, Bucky."

Bucky didn't like this news. He didn't

want notoriety. He'd come to Arizona to live a clean life, not to become a gunfighter.

"I guess you've got some real gunfighters here, huh?" he said.

"We don't lack for them. There's the Earps, you know. They're mostly hot air, though. Ben Thompson made all the Earp clan back down, back in Dodge City a few years ago."

John Clum counted the gunmen on his fingers. "The five Earps, counting the half-brother who deals faro in the Stud Horse Bar. Doc Holliday, the gink who claims he was once a dentist back in Tennessee or some such southern state. Doc Holliday sides with the Earps."

Bucky had heard of these men, having read of their exploits when a mere boy back in Virginia.

"Bat Masterson's here, too. He's a lone wolf, though. He's a newspaper man, you know — or was back East before he turned gunman. You'll like talking to him. He's a smart man, and don't sell him short at any time."

Bucky nodded. "Ben Thompson told a reporter in Abilene, Kansas, that in his estimation Bat Masterson is the fastest gunman around, and then Bat paid Ben the same compliment."

"Both of them put the run on Wild Bill Hickok before Wild Bill got murdered up in the Black Hills. When do you want to start work, Bucky?"

"Right now's okay with me, Mr. Clum."

Clum smiled. "You can drop the Mr., Bucky. You're twenty-one. I'm only a few years older than you."

"How'd you know my age, John?"

Clum spread his ink-stained hands. "The report that came in about the gunfight with those Texans gave your age."

"I don't know if I can ever live down that gunfight. I'm afraid it might make people think I'm a gun-toting, pistol-fighting fool with a draw as fast as a rattlesnake is supposed to strike."

"What would be wrong with that?"

"Somebody might deliberately pick trouble with me. Wild Bill said his greatest thorn was gents who wanted to draw against him just to see if they could kill him before he killed them."

Clum smiled. "I suppose there are such egotistic idiots in the world. The longer I live the more foolish I believe mankind becomes, but it's hard to imagine a man so loco he'd risk his life just to prove he could outshoot a well-known gunman."

Bucky later wrote that he'd never seen a town as tough as Tombstone. Tombstone was the shaggy wolf of all frontier bad towns, he later said. Tombstone sat night and day on its ridge and howled at the sun first and then the moon, and when there was no moon it howled at the stars, and when no moon and stars it just howled to be howling.

Bucky was at long last seeing history in the making. This was not sedate old Virginia with the bluebloods riding to the foxes. This was Arizona Territory that needed only good neighbors and plenty of water, the two prime necessities of Hell itself.

This was raw material from which to forge creative short stories or even a novel, if a man had time to write anything but newspaper copy — and copy he did pour out, much to his young boss' satisfaction.

Prospector Ed Schieffelin discovered the Tombstone silver mines in 1877, two years before Bucky came to Arizona Territory. Two years later the townsite was laid out.

Bucky found himself rubbing shoulders with the great and the near-great. He soon discovered that underneath the surface Tombstone roiled with as much activity as it did above to the naked eye.

He soon discovered, also, that John Clum was not the apparently easy going man he pretended to be. Underneath, Clum was a schemer, working solely for his own advancement.

Tombstone was divided into two baser elements, some of these constituents being outright criminals wanted by the Law in more organized parts of the United States.

Clum and the Earps worked hand in hand. With the Earps was the consumptive dentist turned gunman, cadaverous Doc Holliday. When Bucky arrived the hot mayor election was taking shape. Clum was running on the Progressive Ticket, which was elected.

The mayor had control of sale of all lots owned by the city. Many of these lots in the rapidly expanding business section were of course worth small fortunes. Later it was discovered that Clum, as Tombstone mayor, had signed some of these lots over to the Earp brothers, who hung around and gambled and, contrary to popular opinion, apparently never wore a badge while in Tombstone, for no official records are available today showing any Earp on the Tombstone public payroll.

Bucky, of course, stayed shy of Tombstone's politics, for although he was a man's man, crookedness within or outside of the law went against his grain. He did his reporting and had his circle of friends and wrote short stories or verse every possible chance he got. While in Tombstone he sold his first short story, a fact which opened up great visions of authorship for him.

He worked slightly over a year with Clum. During that year the Earps and Holliday fought it out with the Clantons and McLowrys in what became known as the Gunfight in the OK Corral.

Bucky never called it a fight. He dubbed it a massacre with the Earps and Holliday massacring unarmed men, as it was later proved the Clanton and McLowry boys were.

He interviewed Johnny Ringo after the OK Corral affair. "They just walked down there and killed them off," the tall gunslinger said. "They knew Billy Clanton and his bunch were unarmed and they saw a chance to murder them. Had it been me or Curly Bill Brocius who'd killed in cold blood — against defenseless men, too — the whole town would be out chasin' us down."

Bucky knew that the Earps dared not tackle Ringo, for the tall smiling young man was a killer. He had seen Ringo in action. He had, in fact, one day had a shooting contest with Johnny.

Johnny had won by what Johnny called "a powdersmoke whisker, if gunpowder has whiskers, which I doubt." They'd been in Tombstone's dump shooting at tin cans. Bucky put four bullets in his can, tossing it in the air, then missed the fifth.

His can, of course, began to fall, and he shot his last cartridge, his big .45 belching and kicking, but he missed the falling can.

"Four out of six," Johnny mused.

"Not bad for a beginner, Bucky. Here goes my can, *amigo!*"

Johnny threw up a can smaller than the one Bucky had thrown. Bucky watched the master gunman carefully. He soon saw why Johnny Ringo's gun went unchallenged by the Earps, who fancied themselves gunmen.

No sooner had the can left Johnny's right hand than his gun leaped into it. He sent his first bullet into the can before it had reached its zenith. He sank to one knee, fanning his .45 in true gunman fashion, his palm flashing over the hammer so fast his bullets sounded as one continuous roar.

Bucky stared in wonder and admiration. The can leaped, turned over, leaped again; six times the big six-shooter spat lead. Six times the can jumped. When it landed, there wasn't much left.

Ringo got to his feet, automatically loading. Bucky asked, "What made you faster than I?"

"I think I'm faster because I fan. You pull and each time you shoot you have to steady your pistol again and take aim. I just keep my pistol pointed at the can —

keep it stiff and level — and my palm does the rest.''

''I think you're right.''

Johnny taught Bucky how to really aim a short-gun. ''You lay your index finger along the barrel like this with your middle finger hooked around your trigger, like this.''

''Yes, and then?''

''Well, you point toward your target with your index finger. You point at what you aim to hit and your gun lies along your finger, following your point of aim. Try it.''

Bucky drew and leveled, index finger lying level along his gun's barrel, his middle finger pulling the trigger. He and Johnny shot at an ace of spades nailed to a tree quite a distance away.

Bucky shot fast and he hit the card. He looked at his gun and asked, ''Where'd you learn that, Ringo?''

''I heard that Billy the Kid shot in that manner. John Wesley Hardin aimed the same way. John's in Huntsville prison now — over in Texas — making horsehair into bridles and cinchas and things like that. He got convicted and was sent to prison for life for killing that deputy, you know. What was that deputy's name now?" John Ringo's handsome face showed a frown.

"Charlie Webb."

"That's it. Charlie Webb. You've got a good memory, Bucky."

"Newspaper men have to. Without it they're out of business."

"You seem serious today. Something wrong, friend?"

Bucky looked at the lonely Dragoon mountains, lonely and blue in the distance. "Hell's going to break loose soon in town," he said.

Johnny Ringo laughed. "Hell's already broke loose. Stages being robbed of bullion, a big political fight going on for control of town property, this murder in the OK Corral. Your paper seemed to treat it as though the Earps were in the right. You write the story?"

Bucky nodded, face downfallen.

"You wrote a very one-sided point of view, in my opinion, I say that friend to friend, O'Neill. You never saw the Earps murder the Clantons and McLowrys, did you?"

"No, I didn't."

"The Earps saw to it there were hardly any eyewitnesses and those there favored Clum and the Earps. I never saw it either but I've sure got different versions of it than the one you published."

Bucky finally said, "I wrote the copy. Clum edited it. When it got in print it was the way Clum wanted it. He'd changed about everything I wrote."

"You jump him about it?"

"Not yet." Bucky still stared at the blueline mountains. "Hell, Johnny, it's his paper. He owns it. He's responsible for its contents. I only work there, you know."

"But it makes you look like you're a liar, Bucky. Pardon my saying that, but that's the way it looks to me."

"Yes, and to me, too," Bucky said.

CHAPTER 5

Bucky faced John Clum within a few days. "Why don't I just bring in facts and then you write the story?"

Clum looked up from a letter he was reading. "You're objecting to my editing of your stories, O'Neill?"

O'Neill now, not the familiar *Bucky*. "I am, especially in that story about that OK Corral affair last week."

"What about it?"

"I interviewed every eyewitness I could find. I wrote what I considered an unbiased bit of news writing. I put no personal opinion in the story. Yet when it was sold on the street it wasn't my story at all."

"Okay, go on."

"You put personal opinion in it. This opinion favored the Earp faction because you and the Earps are such good friends."

Clum was pale with anger. He looked up, blue eyes sharp. "You don't want to work for me any more, huh, O'Neill? That's what you're trying to tell me?"

"You're right," Bucky immediately said.

Tombstone held nothing for Bucky O'Neill after he and John Clum parted ways. He had a hunch Tombstone was soon to blow up due to political pressure and water seepage into the deep mines that produced silver as the main product and gold and lead and mercury as by-products.

An engineer friend of his had told him on the quiet that one mine was getting quite a bit of water in it and miners in that mine had quit digging one certain direction for if they dug that way engineers were afraid the mine would be completely inundated and no pumps in the world would be big enough to put an underground river dry.

The Earps were also becoming too dangerous. Unless you were a friend of theirs or of one of their friends — such as John Clum — nobody could prophesy what would happen to you.

The town had divided itself into two definite factions: the Earps versus Tombstone's other political faction. Bucky O'Neill knew that in leaving Tombstone he was running from nothing. He had nothing at stake in Tombstone.

He returned to Phoenix. Within a few days he was in the office of United States Circuit Judge D. H. Pinney, an Ohioan who had been appointed to the Arizona Bench by the federal government, inasmuch as Arizona was still a territory and not a state.

Judge Pinney needed a legal secretary. He'd made his headquarters in Prescott, a small mountain village some hundred miles northwest of Phoenix.

Prescott at that time was also the territorial capital. It had been territorial capital from 1864 until 1867, and in 1877 had again become the capital.

Prescott was much cooler summertimes than Phoenix, for Prescott was in the pines and mountains at about a mile altitude while Phoenix was located down on the desert about twelve hundred feet high.

Having been called northwest to

Prescott on business for Charlie McClintock, who now was in poor health down in Phoenix and who now still owned and operated the Phoenix *Herald,* Bucky had been there prior to his tryout for the court reporter job.

Bucky liked Prescott with its high clean cool air and its valley surrounded by pine-clad mountains. Although he didn't know it at that time, the rest of his rather short life would be spent in Prescott although Prescott lost its territorial capital to Phoenix in 1889.

Now let us look at Bucky O'Neill, transplanted Virginian, as he galloped across a mountain park high with Arizona beargrass on this second of February, Ground Hogs Day in 1882.

This day was his birthday. He'd just finished his twenty second year of life. Although he did not know it, of course, he'd already lived more than half his days he'd been allotted on this earth.

He had reached full height, about five feet ten. He had wide shoulders and hours in the saddle had given him the thin waist and slightly bowed legs of a horseman.

His new blue chambray shirt wrinkled in

the mountain breeze. His new brown trousers blended into the darker brown of his used saddle.

He rode a spirited blue-roan horse that would be with him many years — many years when comparing the years of a horse with the years of a man. Big silver rowels of his *sonora* spurs jangled in cadence to the dancing sounds of his horse's shod hoofs on Arizona granite.

He had the strength of a young Missouri mule and was just as healthy. He was afraid of no living man. He was not overbearing nor was he too meek. He would fight to his death for his principles.

He had the strange reputation of being a fearless gunman, a heller with a short-gun, yet he'd never killed a man. He'd wounded his adversaries and not shot to kill.

His present goal in life was to own an Arizona newspaper like Charles McClintock did down in Phoenix. He'd saved slightly over two hundred dollars while working for John Clum down in Tombstone.

He had made up his mind to save every cent he possibly could and eventually own that contemplated newspaper. Arizona was now his home. He longed occasionally to see his parents and brothers and sisters but this was not an overwhelming wish, for he was a mature man under the bright Arizona sun.

Two days later he appeared newly-barbered and cleanly garbed at Prescott's old adobe court house to try out for the shorthand examination. He felt sure that very few people in Arizona knew how to write shorthand and he hoped he would be the only applicant.

To his surprise, four other applicants were seated waiting in the small chamber. He learned that two were soldiers from nearby Fort Whipple and two were civilian clerks also at the same army post near Prescott.

He realized he faced tough competition. Three of the men had attended some college and one was a college graduate. He'd practiced shorthand for a week prior to the interview and he'd always used shorthand to transcribe his notes during his newspaper career.

What had appeared a cinch but a few moments ago now looked like a tough struggle.

Circuit Judge Pinney did not test the applicants. He left that to a federal employee who traveled throughout the West just to administer examinations for federal positions.

Each applicant was interviewed and tested in a separate room from the others. The clerk, of course, asked questions about the applicant's scholastic education and marks earned therein.

Bucky fell down not an iota in this questioning. He proudly related that he had a law degree and had a license to practice in Washington, D. C., and he had with him the necessary papers to prove both claims valid.

The clerk's well-trained eyebrows rose slightly. Undoubtedly he thought it odd that an individual who could practice law in Washington, D. C., was out hiding in Arizona brush doing newspaper work and gunning down an occasional man, but he discreetly said nothing on these two points.

The government worker then read rapidly from Charles Dickens' *Tale of Two Cities,* and Bucky's pencil skimmed over paper just as rapidly as the clerk could read. Bucky knew he'd missed not a word and that his shorthand was very legible and easy for the clerk to read.

Bucky was the second tested and he took a brief walk in the cooling pines while he waited for final results. Finally, the last of the five came from the testing room and, one hour later, the final selection was made, the clerk clearing his throat.

He had graded papers on two levels of equal importance, he told the five applicants. One level was based on amount and type of education the applicant had received.

Bucky silently thanked Captain John O'Neill and his good mother for making him get a college degree.

The other basis of evaluation was made on the rapidity and accuracy each applicant had achieved in the shorthand test.

The clerk paused. Bucky tried to swallow. His throat was too dry. He really wanted this high paying job. He really needed this job. He breathed deeply and the clerk continued in his high nasal voice.

Three applicants had not successfully transcribed the passages the clerk had read for the shorthand test. Bucky thought, *It's between some person and me in this room,* and impatiently waited, throat progressively becoming drier and drier.

The clerk continued. The two persons who had successfully passed the shorthand test had been judged solely upon educational qualifications. Bucky shifted, wishing the clerk would end the suspense.

"The winner is William Owen O'Neill," the clerk said. "I thank you other gentlemen and wish you luck if you undergo other governmental examinations. This way, please, Mr. O'Neill."

Bucky found Judge Pinney easy to work for. He soon discovered that His Honor did not dislike Arizona. Judge Pinney *loathed* Arizona.

Bucky soon learned that the good judge always compared Arizona Territory with his home state of Ohio.

The northern half of Arizona was worthless because it had no farm land, Judge Pinney said. The second half was worthless because it was all sand and desert, rattlesnakes and scorpions, and boiling heat in summer and drifting snow and sand in winter.

Bucky did not point out that the Hashknife cow-outfit ran thousands and thousands of head in the Tonto Basin and under the Mogollon Rim and that sheepmen had flocks of ten thousand under one herder.

Nor did he mention to the judge that farmers were building checkdams in both the Salt and Gila Rivers and were beginning to make the desert bloom like the proverbial rose around Phoenix and Yuma, respectively.

Judge Pinney lamented the fact that the United States had ever annexed Arizona Territory after buying it from Mexico. He said that keeping army posts such as Prescott's Fort Whipple was a complete waste of the people's money, for in his opinion Arizona should still belong to the roving Apaches and Navajos and other Arizona Indian tribes.

Again Bucky did not disagree or raise contrary points. His job was not to argue the merits — or demerits — of his adopted country. He would be glad when finally Arizona was admitted to the Union as a state with a state's many privileges, for as a territory Arizona was only a stepson to the other states.

He was saving every cent he could for his newspaper. This didn't mean that he didn't have an occasional drink with the others on Saturday night or occasionally date some pretty town girl.

Unlike most other Western men who became famous and fast-draw lawmen, Bucky O'Neill wasted very little time in saloons with the rougher pioneer element. He did not hold the rougher element in scorn. He accepted them and their foibles and strengths as a necessary part of humanity.

One reason he never went much to drinking emporiums was because his stomach just couldn't hold down alcohol. He wrote that alcohol almost invariably made him not drunk but sick, and who would drink just to become ill?

As for the girls . . . ah, that was a different matter. Always courteous in a manner bespeaking of his gentle and proper rearing, he became very, very popular with the young Arizona belles, many of whom considered him as good a *catch* as did their over-anxious mothers.

Although Judge Pinney's home bailiwick was the Prescott area the good judge moved from town to town to hold court, with Bucky, of course, accompanying him. The judge, though, usually went by covered landau, four head of government mules pulling the rig, a coachman — usually a Fort Whipple private — seated in the open on the high driver's seat.

Bucky didn't ride with the judge, for that would not have been fitting and proper; besides, Bucky wanted to see as much of this land as he could — therefore he rode his roan and, if his supplies were too heavy or too many or too bulky to tie behind his saddle, he loaded them on a pack mule which he either led or chased ahead of him.

Judge Pinney held court in whatever building the town provided for him. A few times, to Bucky's amusement, court was held in saloons.

Bucky usually sat at a table below the judge's bench, pencil rapidly transcribing in shorthand. Then, after court was finished for the day, he put this shorthand into correct, neat, legible longhand into an official judicial record.

Bucky found his legal training coming to good stead for Judge Pinney loved to throw out highly legalized phrases that left his court spectators looking from one to the other in hopes of receiving an explanation of what His Honor had just stated.

That same summer Charles McClintock dropped dead working his old Washington press and upon Bucky, Charles' best friend, fell the task of making funeral arrangements.

Mrs. McClintock knew nothing about business and wanted Bucky to run the *Herald* but Bucky politely declined, not mentioning that the next paper he ran would, he hoped, be his own property.

Charles had two good newspaper men working for him and between them they got enough cash to buy the *Herald,* something Bucky had not wanted to do had he had the money — for he wanted to make cool Prescott and not boiling hot Phoenix his center of operations.

Besides, he was very much interested in a certain young lady in Prescott. Her folks said she shouldn't marry for some time and, because Bucky admired this girl's father and mother, he decided to abide by their decision. And perhaps it was best to get to know the girl very well before marrying her. For, as the girl's father joked, there'd be no divorces if there'd be no marriages so, carrying this logic on further, was not marriage then the cause of divorce?

All this was in fun, of course, but underneath had run a vein of serious honesty, for both mother and father of the girl loved her very much — and therefore wanted the best for their lovely young daughter.

And Bucky, being serious, wanted the same for her. Also, because of his government job, he traveled much and spent weeks and weeks out of Prescott following Judge Pinney on His Honor's judicial rounds.

He also intended to start his newspaper in Prescott, although the mountain town already had one weekly.

Things were not dull on the court circuit, though. In September in 1883 court was held in Mineral Springs, a mining town. Bucky had to make it to Mineral Springs before court convened at ten in the morning.

He now owned three saddle horses which he pastured adjoining Prescott. This particular day he was astraddle his four-year-old sorrel mare.

Two miles from Mineral Springs he was loping through the pines when suddenly and without warning he was flying forward through the air, his horse doubling under him as she fell.

He landed on the hard ground on his left shoulder and then he sat up sick with shock, wondering what the mare had fallen over.

She'd caught the tip of her right front shoe on a root, he noticed. The mare had scrambled to her feet and now stood with trailing reins awaiting him, ears pricked forward.

Bucky realized his new silk shirt was torn and his left arm hung limply. He decided his arm was broken just below the shoulder.

Teeth gritted against pain, he unloosened his belt and, somehow, slipped his arm under it, cinching the belt down again so the arm wouldn't dangle. He was drenched with cold sweat. Never had he thought a broken arm could bring its owner such excruciating pain.

The thought came that he was fortunate that his right arm had not been broken for his right arm was essential in his court reporting. He went to his mare, every step sending pain through his arm and shoulder.

He found difficulty in mounting so he led the mare to a nearby stump where she patiently stood while he got into saddle. He put the mare toward Mineral Springs, discovering she limped badly from her fall.

Mare and rider limped into Mineral Springs ten minutes before court was due to convene. Judge Pinney offered to postpone court for a week but Bucky said he could transcribe yet for his right hand was still good, wasn't it?

The judge then slyly intimated that certain mountain streams adjacent to Mineral Springs contained some fine trout fishing and he was anxious to prove if reports he'd heard of this great fishing were true or not.

Bucky grinned, understanding.

When court was finally convened the next week Bucky had his left arm in a sling and Judge Pinney had proven that certain mountain streams near Mineral Springs, Territory of Arizona, indeed lived up to trout fishing claims he'd heard.

Bucky's job needed more than transcribing finesse, though, for in some areas of Arizona justice was not accomplished in courts but by gunsmoke and fistfights, some of the latter becoming gang fights which left wounded or dead behind.

Bucky arrived at the opinion that the Territory needed a militia that could be sent out by the Territorial Governor to quell riots such as that now brewing in the Tonto Basin where men — and even women — fought to the bloody end over practically no reason.

Once Judge Pinney held court in a desert town to decide which of two men owned a certain waterhole they'd been fighting about, for water on the desert was worth more than its weight in gold. Water was life, human or animal or vegetable.

The desert had seen no rain for months.

This was one of the longest dry spells seen even by the oldest Apache in this section.

The two cattlemen doing the fighting had many friends and relatives to back each's claim to the precious water. Feeling ran high in the false-fronted cowtown flung out on Arizona's limitless southern desert.

Judge Pinney spent two days in selecting what he hoped would be an unbiased jury of twelve men. Each cowman had hired big-name lawyers from Phoenix and the first day passed with these high-paid barristers interrogating witnesses.

Angry rumblings occasionally ran through the onlookers and witnesses who watched the lawyers — and witnesses — very, very carefully. Bucky sensed trouble ahead if certain witnesses gave certain answers derogatory to the cause of either or both cattlemen.

The second day saw the small building crowded to bursting with townspeople, cowboys, miners and ranchers. The attorneys, waxing hot and eloquent, drifted from the subject at hand and began insulting each other's integrity and ability as a barrister.

Bucky scowled. Judge Pinney pounded his gavel, but the thing had gone too far. It became a fight not over water but over the personalities of the barristers concerned.

Finally one lawyer, unable to control his rage, grabbed an inkwell from a desk and threw it at another barrister, ink flying all directions . . . and the fight was on!

Desperately, Judge Pinney gaveled and hollered for order, but all in vain. Nothing but a territorial militia could have averted the trouble that followed.

Bucky's first allegiance was to Judge Pinney, who was past middle-age. Accordingly, fists slugging, Bucky worked his way over to the judge, who stood behind his makeshift lectern, face pale with rage as he desperately called for order to prevail.

Seeing his pounding and shouting was of no avail, Judge Pinney threw his gavel aside and doubled his fists, starting forward. Bucky knew His Honor did not lack courage. Judge Pinney had achieved an enviable war record in the Civil War.

But he was no longer a young man, and Bucky grabbed him unceremoniously, reminding him of that fact. Judge Pinney sighed and then just stood and watched, doubled hands resting on his makeshift lectern while the battlers struggled around him, Bucky O'Neill now one of them.

For a big cowboy had slugged Bucky behind the right ear. Bucky saw a momentary collection of stars and then he'd gone to work, mowing the cowboy down with first a hard left to the midsection, then a right flush on the granite jaw.

The cowboy went sailing back into the shouting, cursing, fighting mob, later to come to and crawl out the front door, wondering just what mule had kicked him before remembrance returned.

Jury members had first thrown chairs at the combatants but, running out of chairs, had leaped the rail and plunged in, fists working as they shouted obscenities.

Even screaming women joined the battle, some engaging in hair-pulling royal, others using the jurors' chairs as clubs. Bucky then discovered, to his amazement, that some women could curse better than their men.

Tables crashed to the floor. Combatants

fell over the tables and broken chairs. Windows broke as wood and men and women flew through them. Men went down knocked unconscious.

Bucky knocked one of the cattlemen flying through the mob. A cowboy started a haymaker that Bucky didn't see even after it landed hard on his jaw, staggering him and almost dropping him.

Bucky never got a chance to tangle with the cowboy. A miner clipped the bronc-rider on the jaw from the left side and dropped him like a heart-shot deer.

Bucky fought over to where the town marshal was trying to tear two women apart. "We got to stop this, marshal," Bucky called.

"Yeah," the marshal sourly hollered in return. "You tell me how, O'Neill, and I'll stop it. Mrs. Hannigan, please! Mrs. Myers is your next door neighbor and you two have been friends for years and years —"

Bucky slugged a businessman in the belly, doubling him in pain, for the man had another merchant by the ears, pushing his head down floorward. "You will undersell me huh, you bastard," the businessman gritted just as Bucky knocked him down.

Bucky hoped no gunfire would boom out in this struggling mass of enraged humanity. Although he and the marshal had searched each person entering the court a gun might be thrown in through a broken window or the door or a gun might have entered despite precautions.

He grabbed the businessman who'd been grabbed by the ears. "We've got to stop this, man," he gritted, "or somebody might get killed."

"This has gone beyond a fight for water," the man panted, sleeving blood from his nose. "Everybody in town is here to settle old scores."

"A minute or so ago you were a reliable, law-abiding citizen," Bucky yelled. "Now you've gone crazy. This community looks to you for leadership — not cheap barroom fighting and —"

Bucky had noticed that the businessman had gone deadly pale. He stared at a point behind Bucky, who whirled in time to see a long Bowie knife upraised, the shiny knife held in a grim big cowboy fist.

The cowboy had smuggled the knife in

someway, Bucky hurriedly realized. Then the knife lanced down, wicked and razor-sharp. It buried itself to the hilt in the other cowboy's arching chest.

The knifed cowboy died with a gurgling scream. Bucky's blood went ice cold at the sight of the bloody upraised knife.

He grabbed the remains of a chair. He threw it desperately at the knifeman. By sheer luck the chair caught the enraged man in the face.

The man staggered back. Within an instant, Bucky was behind the knifeman, both arms around the killer as he grabbed the man by both wrists, his powerful fingers digging into the man's forearm.

The cowboy was bigger than Bucky and stronger. Bucky fought to retain his hold, the knife poised in the man's bloody fingers. Bucky finally got his left knee buried in the man's spine.

With a desperate heave, Bucky put all his waning strength into his arms, and threw the man over his head, much as he'd thrown the rough named Red Hopkins down in Tucson, almost two years ago.

The cowboy went over Bucky's left

shoulder. He dropped his knife which the marshal immediately leaped upon.

The sight of cold steel — and deadly murder — had stopped the combatants. Old scores had been settled. Some were so tired they couldn't lift their arms. Now all stared at the man behind Bucky.

Bucky whirled and made a football tackle, pinning the cowboy to the floor. The cowboy fought with savage ferocity. He was getting loose, despite Bucky's efforts.

He was just too much for the smaller Bucky. The cowboy fairly threw Bucky aside and leaped to his feet, intent on fleeing — but he got but a few feet for a pistol rang out suddenly in the small room, sending the murderer toppling again onto the floor.

This time, the cowboy didn't rise. He moaned, eyes closed, lips compressed, right hand grabbing his left shoulder. Bucky saw blood cover his hand. He looked at the marshal who stood with a smoking pistol and a wounded look on his homely visage.

"I hated to shoot him." The marshal's voice was dull and faraway. "He is my friend."

"Watch the back door," Bucky ordered. "Let nobody out. I'll take the front. Hurry, marshal."

The town doctor, who'd been in the fight, now knelt beside the wounded man, peeling back the cowboy's bullet-holed shirt and swabbing the wound with a handkerchief which soon was brilliant red.

"Broken collarbone," he said, getting to his feet. "I'll need him in my office."

"What about Jim Hicks?" a woman asked.

The doctor looked at the knifed man. "He's dead," he said. "That knife entered his heart. I saw that at one glance."

The marshal and a merchant took the wounded man to the doctor's office, where he was treated and confined later to the town jail — a one-cell affair behind the courthouse.

Judge Pinney called court to order. He delivered a stern, tight-lipped lecture and then fined each attorney five hundred and costs, payable immediately, and if no attorney had the five hundred on him he'd be locked in jail nights until the money arrived.

One lawyer — the inkwell thrower — rose to object to such stiff fines and Judge Pinney ordered him taken to jail immediately. Two townsmen gleefully jumped to the task, each with torn shirts and bloody faces.

The jurist then fined every combatant — including all the women — fifty dollars and costs. One woman opened her mouth to object and His Honor immediately sentenced her to two days in jail and ordered two men to carry her to the jail where she'd be thrown in with the lawyer, a chaperon sitting between them.

The sentencing of the lawyer and the townswife quieted the group. Those who had the money on their persons paid their fines and costs immediately but those who didn't have the fifty dollars had to pay as much as they could now and pay the remainder within forty-eight hours or go to jail.

Bucky was busy registering names and addresses of those who couldn't pay. His right knuckles had been skinned and writing was somewhat difficult but in time the courtroom was cleared and only he and Judge Pinney were in the small room.

"I suppose I didn't make myself too popular," His Honor said, "but law and order must be maintained. Unless they are anarchy holds a nation and life is in danger continuously."

Bucky found a mop and a bucket which he filled at the pump behind the building. He mopped the blood from the floor. The dead man had been taken to the town morgue.

Judge Pinney had adjourned court for thirty-six hours. Next day he called on the town's residents, going from business to business, house to house. Bucky continued busily collecting fines.

At the end of the adjournment limit Judge Pinney again called court to session where the jury, some of them with black eyes and split lips, decided neither cowman had clear title to the water in question, thus throwing the waterhole open to public use.

Judge Pinney then bound the killer over to the fall term of court in Phoenix and he and Bucky left town, a small fortune in fines resting in the pack on Bucky's mule traveling ahead of His Honor's landau.

Bucky rode fitting his saddle, thinking

about His Honor's last words back in the pioneer cowtown as Judge Pinney had stepped into his rig.

"These people are like people all over the world," the judge had said. "They are barbarians at heart. Lawyers are supposed to be controlled, learned men — but lawyers started this fighting."

Bucky could only nod.

He remembered saying goodby to the marshal.

"I've known most of these people all my life," the lawman had said. "I never knew so much hate could ever be inside of them. They acted like stampeding cattle. The minute that lawyer threw that inkwell they were off slugging."

"What if they'd rushed the doors before you and I blocked them, marshal? What would have then happened?"

"They'd have taken to hiding, I guess. It would have taken a band of mounted men to run some down."

"That's what this territory needs," Bucky said.

"What does it need?" the marshal asked.

"A band of mounted lawmen."

CHAPTER 6

The July day had been very hot but now that the sun had set behind the pines a cooling mountain twilight blessed this section of Arizona Territory. Dust rose from Fort Whipple's parade grounds as Bucky O'Neill, mounted on a big gray horse, directed his Prescott Grays in a drill exercise.

Six weeks had passed since the killing of the cowboy by the knifeman, and two weeks after returning to Prescott Bucky had organized this militia mounted band.

Bucky's next court session wouldn't start for six months, although his federal paycheck came in the first of each month, regardless. He therefore had much time for his writing and his newly-organized mounted posse.

A neat gray uniform graced his

muscular body. The thirty mounted riders of his also wore immaculate gray and each was astride a gray gelding, each gelding being about the same color of gray and weighing about the same.

Judge Pinney had sworn Bucky's men into this unit, each rider agreeing to instantly ride to enforce territorial laws when called upon in an emergency.

This was the Grays' first chance to enjoy a full-dress parade, for uniforms had arrived only this morning; the uniforms had been bought by townsmen and local merchants.

The Grays consisted of local men and surrounding cowboys. All morning housewives and Prescott's one tailor had been busy making minor alterations on the uniforms to insure their correct fit.

Bucky realized he was not a good cavalry commander. He wished his father had been on hand to give him instructions on drilling cavalry, but Captain John was far away in Virginia, ailing from age and the effects of his many Civil War bullet wounds.

Bucky had hastily boned-up on cavalry procedure through books the *commandante* of Fort Whipple had thoughtfully loaned him. Fort Whipple sergeants had also taught him cavalry commands.

Fort Whipple was older than Prescott, having been established before the town was formed. Some claimed that had there been no Fort Whipple undoubtedly there'd now be no Prescott, for Prescott was built to accommodate the cavalrymen stationed at Fort Whipple.

With the Apaches now securely on reservations, there was some talk about abandoning the fort.

Fort Whipple's *commandante* had gladly given Bucky permission to stage his Grays' drills on the fort's parade ground. "This territory needs a militia, Bucky," the grizzled Indian fighter had said. "Now if you can get the bigwigs in Washington to appoint your group the territory's official militia you've got it in the bag, son."

"I'm working on that angle now, sir."

"You can drill on our parade ground whenever it's not occupied and that's about every afternoon for we drill only once a week and then in the mornings. Good luck, son."

"Thank you, General."

Now the Grays moved ahead, stopped, wheeled, stood horses at attention, and went through various cavalry movements, some of Fort Whipple's "horse-soldiers" calling good-natured advice from the sidelines, where just about every soul in Prescott watched and cheered.

Most people had walked the short distance from town but some had come in buggies, springwagons, lumberwagons and on mules and horses. Now Bucky grinned, raised a hand, and called, "Fall out, riders. Company dismissed."

A cheer went up from the spectators, even from a cavalry sergeant friend of Bucky's — a man who'd served with General Miles in Montana Territory against the Sioux and Northern Cheyenne.

"You seem extra happy today, Bucky. Something nice happen, maybe?"

Bucky leaned low from saddle. "I sold another short story today back East. That makes my fifth sale."

"Wheew, that's good. Pay you much?"

"The five sales combined paid me more than a year's wages on my secretary job."

"Good again. Why not just write

for a living?"

"I'm thinking of that, but first I hope to own a weekly newspaper. I guess printer's ink is in my blood."

Bucky and his Grays mailed out stories to all the territory's newspapers boasting the Grays and explaining why they were organized. Bucky had gained much notoriety because of the Texans down in Phoenix but by this time that was almost forgotten.

Once again the name of William Owen O'Neill, alias Bucky O'Neill, stared out at territorial citizens from territorial newspapers, but this was definitely not the last time that name would see print throughout all of Arizona.

Bucky mused about his projected newspaper. He felt sure a newspaper that contained solely local and national interest would not have a wide distribution, for the Territory already had such newspapers.

He realized that cattle-raising as an industry grew bigger each passing year in Arizona. One night while undressing for bed the idea hit him. He just sat there, one shoe in hand, mouth agape — and realized that the idea was a very simple one and why hadn't he thought of it before?

Cattlemen had no newspaper devoted solely to their profession. Next morning Bucky swallowed his pride and talked about a loan to the local banker, a member of his Grays.

The banker listened carefully at first and then patiently toward the end and Bucky knew he'd lost before he was one-third into his spiel.

"Papers are supported not by circulation sales but by advertising income," the banker reminded, "and from where will come your advertisers?"

Bucky knew full well what the banker inferred. The local weekly newspaper had been established when Prescott had been founded and now was owned by the son of the original founder.

This man naturally had all local advertising corralled, for his was the only advertising medium in Prescott.

"Do you think you can pull local advertisers away from Fred Biggons?" the banker said. "If you can't, then you'll not succeed with a contemplated newspaper because local merchants don't do enough volume business to support two newspapers."

Bucky got to his feet. "I've got to come up with a better one than that, huh?"

The banker nodded. "Sorry, Bucky, but I can't underwrite you. If I did my trustees would fire me for incompetency."

Bucky went to his boarding house, dubbed Fort Starvation by its occupants, and sat on his bed in his small room and did some more thinking. Finally his rugged face brightened.

The bank was closed so that evening he went to the banker's home and outlined his plan.

"Okay, Hank, okay. I believe I've come up with the answer. Let's say that a man over in Maricopa County starts raising cattle."

"Go ahead."

"We'll give this fictitious man the name of Thomson, without a p. He wants to use his initial, T, in his brand and decides to brand the Circle T on the right ribs."

"Yes?"

"Now let's travel way down southeast in the Territory and find a man named

Turbeck who also wants to start in the cow business — or already is in it — and he brands his stock Circle T, and also on the right ribs."

"A coincidence, but very probable. What's your point, Bucky?"

"Well, cattle stray even hundreds of miles. A Thomson steer strays to Pima County and mixes in with Turbeck's Circle T cattle. So who does the Circle T steer belong to? Turbeck or Thomson?"

Hank shrugged. "To the one on whose range it is found, I'd say, but what are you driving at, O'Neill?"

"Just this," Bucky said, and began explaining.

His idea was to start a newspaper for cattlemen that would also act as the official brand registry office, a service the federal government had been asked to furnish the territory but had always rejected as an unnecessary territorial expenditure.

"First, I register every brand extant in the Territory, Hank. Then I'll be able to tell if there are any duplications like the one we just imagined. If so, the cattlemen can straighten it out among themselves to the betterment of all cowmen concerned.''

"Now you talk business, Bucky. You've got a plan there.''

"And each time a man starts a new brand he submits it to me for official filing. If it duplicates a brand now in existence I'll not register it, of course, and he can concoct a new brand for registration — one that is original in Arizona.''

"That sounds good, too.''

"Now there's another angle, too, Hank. Let's say a steer strays miles from his home range, and you know steers many times do just that.''

"Some stray a hundred or more miles away until they're four-year-olds and ready for the market. Continue.''

"Well, this strayed steer gets big enough to go to market. The man whose range the critter's on has no idea who owns the animal for he doesn't recognize the owner of the steer's brand.''

"Uh-huh, I understand.''

"But the man sells the stray steer and gets the pay for him, because he can't afford to keep the steer until the critter dies of old age. The cowman now has payment for a steer that wasn't his.

"Most cattlemen are honest. Our man would like to pay the money he received for the steer to the steer's legal owner but he can't because he doesn't know who the legal owner is and steers can't talk."

"They sure can't."

"Each Christmas time — or around there — I'd print a list of cattle shipped or sold by cowmen not their owners. I'd list the steer's brand, his color, distinguishing marks like earmarks, his approximate age and price he drew at market."

"Where would you get this information?"

"From my cattlemen subscribers, of course. They'd send it in to me. Then the cowman who legally owned the steer could collect from the cattleman who sold him, the two of them deducting if they wanted the price of feed the steer had eaten on his new range, and things like that."

Hank stroked his chin thoughtfully. "I believe you've got a splendid idea, Bucky. You get enough cowmen to underwrite your newspaper and I'll have to advance you funds. But how will you get the cowmen behind you . . . that is, if they want to get behind you?''

Bucky said, "The cattlemen are holding a territorial meeting next week in Phoenix. I'm going down there and try to read a paper to them or someway get them interested in my plan. There's talk of their creating a Territory of Arizona Stockgrowers Association.''

"I've heard that, too. The Territory needs such a group. We're growing fast, Bucky. If we keep this up we'll finally be a State.''

"I'll charge ten percent commission on all *Lost or Strayed,* acting as middleman between the seller and the owner. That, with advertising and subscriptions, should keep my sheet running.''

"Good luck at the convention, Bucky.''

Bucky rose to his feet, grinning. He had the financial backing now. All he had to do was get cowmen to underwrite what would be *their own* newspaper. He told his future wife about his plans that night while they sat spooning on a bench in the town plaza.

"Oh, Bucky, how I hope *your* dream comes true and becomes *our* dream, darling.''

Bucky smiled. "Dreams don't come true of their own volition. You have to work and plug to make them become reality. I leave for Phoenix in the morning on the stage, honey."

"I'll miss you."

"I've got another plan, too, but it can wait until I get back, because the convention is the main thing."

At first, the cattlemen were not interested in the plan, for cow thievery was heavy, especially in the Tombstone area; this held their attention for the first two days of the four day meeting.

The third day Bucky broached his plan to a few cowmen at a bar, but they expressed little interest. Dismay hit the newspaperman, court reporter, militia leader, and sometime lawman. He went to his hotel room that night completely worn out.

Next morning he approached the program manager and briefly outlined his plan, the man listening politely with a faraway look in his eyes. He said he'd give the plan some thought but didn't definitely promise to put the matter before the convention on this, its last day.

Bucky again read down the list of stockmen scheduled to be at the meeting, and he saw not a name he recognized except a few minor cowmen from around Prescott whom he'd already approached and who had rebuffed him.

He was walking out of the convention hall when a hearty voice said, "By God, if it isn't Bucky O'Neill, the *Epitaph's* past star reporter!"

Bucky turned to his right, for the hearty words had come from a man sitting in a wheelchair almost hidden in the corner. Bucky hurried to the gray-haired man's side and eagerly shook the extended work-calloused hand.

"Matt Watson! From Tombstone, itself. What's the matter, friend? How come you ride that two-wheeled bronc?"

Matt Watson ran thousands of head east of Tombstone and down to the Mexican Border. Bucky had wondered why the name of a cowman this big had not been included in the attendance list.

Watson had had a horse go over backwards with him a year ago, the blow breaking the cowman's left pelvis, and he said doctors claimed he'd never walk

108

again, let alone ride a bronc. Bucky asked why Watson's name had not been included in the attendance list.

Watson explained that the chairman of the stockman's commission had written him about this meeting but he'd written back he'd not been able to make the trip.

"But at the last moment Mom said I should go, sawbones or no sawbones, so here I am. What are you doing here? You gone into the cow business and dropped newspaper work?"

Matt Watson and Bucky had been close friends in Tombstone, having met in John Clum's office when Matt Watson had placed an ad each week for his general store located in Tombstone, for the cowman was also in the mercantile business, along with numerous other business ventures.

"Matt, will you listen to me a while?"

The cowman-merchant-banker looked at him curiously. "Anything you want to say, Bucky, I'm ready to listen to. What's on your mind, son, besides your new white Stetson?"

Sitting there beside the wheelchair, Bucky outlined his plan, Matt Watson gazing at people coming and going, nodding to this one then that, and, when Bucky was finally finished, the cowman-merchant gazed for a moment into space.

Bucky straightened, thinking, I've lost again. The plan isn't any good. This man with his business acumen would know if I could make it pay or not. His face and look show he's not interested.

Then Matt Watson said, "There's only one thing wrong, Bucky, and it's this: why was I so stupid I never thought of such a good thing. It's just what the Territory cowmen need. Have you broached anybody else?"

"Nobody else would listen to me, Matt."

"That's to their misfortune, friend. Just a while ago the chairman asked me if I had something to say and I told him I hadn't but I sure as hell have now. I'll bring it up in the afternoon session but you'll have to do the talking, Bucky."

Bucky mopped his sweating forehead. "That I sure will, Matt, and I don't know how I'll ever thank you."

"You can repay me by marrying that pretty girl you've got in Prescott."

Bucky looked up in surprise. "How'd

you know about Pauline?'' he asked.

Matt Watson boomed his hearty laugh. ''I just hit in the dark. Any man as nice as you are, Bucky, has to have a pretty girl waiting for him, or the women in Prescott would have to have something wrong with them.''

Bucky took the evening stage for Prescott with a note in his pocket signed by Matt Watson and three other big Territory cowmen allowing him up to twenty thousand dollars credit at any bank to which it was presented.

Next morning he showed the certified note, duly and legally notarized, to his friend the banker, who established credit for him to the sum of twenty thousand, and then he went to the Clerk and Recorder's office in the court house and looked into last year's Official Records.

The local newspaper had said last week in an official county notice that bids were now open on the county's printing needs for the coming year, and Bucky soon found out how much the local newspaper had bid in the year past to gain the contract.

Bucky decided to submit the same figure

that the local publisher had submitted last year. He felt sure the publisher would submit a higher bill this year for Prescott had added quite a few new families, all going into official records at the court house.

He told nobody, not even Pauline, about this plan, although he had told her about his letter of credit from Matt Watson and the other three influential cowmen, pledging her to secrecy.

He'd ordered his presses and paper and equipment while in Phoenix, with delivery promised in three weeks which would be the day the contract was awarded for the county printing.

The editor of the local weekly did not even bother to attend the meeting of the county commissioners that would award the county printing contract. Why should he go?

He owned Prescott's only newspaper. County regulations stated that a newspaper in the county had to be awarded the contract. Any newspaper outside of the county could not even submit a bid and, if such a bid were submitted, it would not be accepted.

There were but a few interested taxpayers at the meeting. Legality required that the head commissioner ask if any other bids would be tendered, and to the surprise of all Bucky handed in his bid.

"But you haven't a print shop," the commissioner said.

"If my bid is the lower I'll print everything the county needs," Bucky said.

Bucky's bid was opened. It was almost a thousand dollars below that of his only competitor. He told the commissioners he would be bonded and the money to pay for his bond was in the bank.

"But a man without a printing press. . . ." the head commissioner again said. "Bring in the county attorney to consult on the legality of this, please, bailiff."

The county attorney was stumped. Bucky had looked up the law on this point and he diplomatically explained this to the attorney, pointing out that the law did not state that the bidder had to have a printing press.

The attorney and Bucky then consulted the correct law tome and the attorney said, "In my legal opinion the bid of Mr.

O'Neill must be accepted because it is the lower and because Mr. O'Neill can also furnish bond."

Thus Bucky won the county printing contract. A few days later two heavily-laden freight wagons pulled by six mules each lumbered to a stop in front of a small building Bucky'd rented on Prescott's main street.

Onlookers quickly gathered. The press and supplies had come overland from Los Angeles. Bucky hired extra men on the spot to help get the heavy equipment into the new office which luckily had a durable concrete floor that could stand such ponderous weight.

Bucky noticed the owner of the local newspaper in the watching crowd. He'd heard the man had been very irate about his winning the county printing contract but the newspaperman had not accosted Bucky.

Bucky noticed that his competitor had a long, sour face. Once alone in his new print shop, Bucky walked around his huge beautiful new printing press, eyes shimmering.

The town painter entered. "Got your

new sign out in my springwagon, Bucky. Got a couple of ladders there, too, but I'll need help to hang the sign, because it's pretty heavy.''

The two got the sign hanging onto brackets Bucky had already installed, then braced it solidly with guy wires against wind and storm. Then, hands on hips, Bucky O'Neill stood on the plank sidewalk, proudly gazing up at the big sign.

HOOFS AND HORNS
Bucky O'Neill, Publisher

CHAPTER 7

Mike Murphy was then Prescott's sheriff. Murphy was a patient middle-aged man who'd grown stolid and taciturn under the weighty demands of his office. Two years after Bucky O'Neill had opened his newspaper office, a local rancher strode into Sheriff Murphy's office, rage making his suntanned rugged face pale.

"What's your trouble, John?" Sheriff Murphy asked.

The cowman reported he was sure he was losing cattle to a rustler named Dilda — whether Dilda was the man's last name or first records did not show.

Dilda was a short, dark-complexioned man of about thirty-five. Local people dubbed him a "range bum." He did not work, he owned no property but two head of horses, but he usually had a little

116

money. Already many people were suspicious of him.

"Did you actually see Dilda stealing one of your steers, John?"

John shook his head. "I never saw him in the act, no — but he's ridin' my grass a lot an' I'm just losin' too many head, Mike."

Sheriff Murphy gave this some thought. "I can't ask the county judge to give me a warrant for Dilda's arrest on such flimsy evidence, John, but I will ride out and talk to Dilda. Where's he holed-up at?"

"He's hangin' out in that ol' minin' shack up on the foot of Thunder Mountain."

"I'll drop by later at your ranch and tell you what happened," the sheriff said, buckling on his spurs.

Sheriff Murphy left town with his black gelding on a trail-lope, waving to his friend Bucky O'Neill, who stood in front of *Hoofs and Horns* talking to his bride, whom the sheriff thought sure was a pretty girl.

Bucky hadn't had time to ask Sheriff Murphy where he was bound for. Accordingly, he kept close to the sheriff's office that day, his newsman's nose telling him a news item might be in the offing.

The undersheriff told him that Sheriff Murphy had gone out to talk to Dilda, who'd been reported as a possible cow thief; Dilda was now holed-up in a shack on Thunder Mountain.

Night came but Sheriff Murphy didn't return. The lawman hadn't returned at midnight. Bucky, worried about his friend, rode out at twelve-thirty that night, heading for Thunder Mountain.

Two hours later he rode into Prescott leading Sheriff Murphy's horse, holding Sheriff Murphy in front of him as he rode behind the cantle of his saddle, the sheriff sagging and bloody in Bucky's arms.

The sheriff had ridden unexpectedly upon Dilda butchering a rustled steer, one stolen from the cowman who'd made the complaint against Dilda.

Dilda had a loaded Winchester rifle leaning close at hand against the dead beef. Pine needles had muffled the hoofsounds of the sheriff's horse. Therefore Dilda hadn't heard the lawman coming.

The moment that Sheriff Murphy rode

into the clearing, Dilda grabbed his rifle. With one sweep, Dilda raised the rifle waist high — and fired twice, his first bullet hitting the sheriff in the chest and knocking him from horse, the second whamming harmlessly into the endless blue of the Arizona sky.

Without a word to the sheriff, the cow thief leaped into his saddle and spurred away, leaving the stolen steer behind in his haste to quit that section.

Sheriff Murphy had been unable to mount but he did manage to crawl to a nearby water hole where Bucky found him, almost unconscious from loss of blood.

Bucky took the sheriff to the court house. The town doctor hurried over, but his services were of no avail. Sheriff Murphy quietly died after swearing a deposition stating true facts about his being shot. Bucky and other townsmen testified as to the dying man's signature.

The big undersheriff buckled on his Cheyenne-legged chaps, his gun tied low on his thigh. "Time I rode out and settled Mr. Dilda's hash," he told Bucky.

Bucky shook his head. "Not alone,

Jake. This a job for my Prescott Grays, friend.'' Bucky spoke to a townsman. ''Get help and get every one of the Grays out of bed and mounted and armed and in front of this courthouse sooner than possible.''

''I'm on my way, Bucky.''

Within half an hour, all the Grays residing in Prescott swept out of town, Bucky heading them on his big gray stud. Those Grays living out of town on ranches would meet the town Grays out on open range.

The Prescott Grays were on their first manhunt, the purpose of their organization. They didn't wear ornate and gaudy dress uniforms now. Each man wore a gray stetson, all stetsons of the small Tom Watson type, and each wore a gray shirt, gray trousers and gray bandanas.

Six-shooters rode their hips. The stocks of Winchester rifles protruded from their saddle-holsters. Their grain-fed tough gray horses pulled at bits, yearning for the thrill of the chase . . . and the trail.

For three long days and nights the mounted band worked, spread out always within shouting distance from each other. Newspaper reporters from the territory rode with them, sending runners back with dispatches. All the United States followed the manhunt in its daily newspapers. The name of Bucky O'Neill became a household name.

The Grays ran Dilda to earth a hundred-odd miles from Prescott, for the man had been stealing horses at different ranches on his wild dash toward the Utah border.

Dilda knew he was vastly outnumbered. He knew that if he made a move toward his pistol or rifle the rifles of the Grays would cut him in half. Wisely, he raised his hands and surrendered without firing a shot.

All of Prescott and most of Northern Arizona was on the Prescott sidewalks to get a look at the killer and cheer the Grays and Bucky as they rode tired, lathered gray broncs into Prescott, their prisoner riding disarmed with hands tied to the horn of his saddle and his boots trussed together by a rope under the belly of his mount.

Dilda was jailed. Bucky feared a jail delivery; thus, he posted two impartial

Grays as guards twenty-four hours a day. Dilda next morning was indicted by the justice-of-the-peace on a murder charge, the man completely caving in when the dead sheriff's deposition was read back to the killer.

"Bucky O'Neill for sheriff," somebody cried.

"Bucky, Bucky, Bucky! Our next sheriff, Bucky O'Neill!"

Pauline said, kissing her husband, "They want you to take Sheriff Murphy's job, darling. I don't really want you to but if you think it best —" Her lovely girlish face showed worry.

For the first time, Bucky realized the severe obligations of matrimony. Were he sheriff and were he to ride out as Sheriff Murphy had done this brown-haired blue-eyed woman — now his wife — would worry and worry about him, just as the bereaved Mrs. Murphy had done when her husband had gone about his lawman obligations.

"A man has to be a man, Pauline," he said gently. "Men need lawmen because most men are evil at heart."

Hoofs and Horns had progressed to the

point where his assistant editor, a young woman, could easily manage it.

The newspaper had grown steadily in circulation the two years it had been in operation. Cowmen all over the Territory — and some in neighboring New Mexico and Utah — had subscribed and used Bucky's brand registry and stray cattle index.

Sometimes the *Hoofs and Horns* had ten thousand dollars or more to send to different cowmen for cattle sold by other cowmen — cattle that had drifted from home range onto range sometimes hundreds of miles away.

Ten percent of this lost or strayed fund kept the newspaper running, and the rest was more or less profit.

Because of *Hoofs and Horns,* Bucky had been forced to resign as Judge Pinney's legal secretary, that position now being held by a former Fort Whipple private who had gone to secretarial school before joining the armed forces.

Bucky realized he'd gone up as far and as high as he could with *Hoofs and Horns,* and therefore the spice was gone from the newspaper's operation. Frankly, the thought of being selected by county commissioners to replace the dead sheriff offered a challenge to him.

Dilda's trial was presided over by Judge Pinney in the fall term of court, curiosity-seekers coming from miles to sit in the jam-packed courtroom or stand back against the wall. Bucky's Grays kept order — it was against regulations to smoke in the courtroom, for a fire would be very serious with so many people present.

Bucky was sergeant-at-arms. Now the Grays wore their town uniforms. The Territory had not as yet selected the Grays as its national militia, but the Territorial Governor had written Bucky a letter commending him and his Grays for capturing Dilda.

The county furnished Dilda with two competent lawyers at a great expense but Dilda had no case and the lawyers knew it. The lawyers finally asked to throw Dilda upon the mercy of the court but Judge Pinney said the man's alleged misdeed was too serious to allow such legal procedure.

Dilda was convicted of first-degree murder. Judge Pinney's court sentenced him to die by hanging, the twelve jurymen sitting stony-faced as their foreman read their verdict.

Dilda was hung the next week and that same day William Owen O'Neill was sworn in as sheriff of Yavapai County, Territory of Arizona, with his headquarters in Prescott, also temporary territorial capital.

Bucky received his oath of office in 1889; therefore, he was twenty-nine years of age — one of the youngest men in Western history to assume the awesome and heavy burdens of a frontier lawman.

His appointment as sheriff to fulfil the rest of the dead Murphy's term, and his subsequent election and re-election, never did sit well with his gentle wife, and apparently was always more or less a bone of contention between the pair, who otherwise had a good and solid marital relationship.

Thus at Dilda's hanging Bucky O'Neill presided as county sheriff and also Captain of the Prescott Grays. Because to him life had many interesting and rewarding days, he disliked seeing Dilda hanged — and he more than once in his career as a police officer stated that he wished the death sentence repealed and replaced by life imprisonment.

So he led the condemned man from the courthouse jail that hot autumn day — his heart pounding perhaps more heavily than that of the condemned man, his Grays standing at stiff attention holding back the crowd as they formed a lane with the ghastly gallows at the far end, the hangman's noose hanging idly over the well-oiled trapdoor that soon would fall and send Dilda plunging into the Hereafter.

Bucky had not handcuffed Dilda. Such a precaution was not necessary with Prescott Grays on either side. Dilda nodded and spoke to acquaintances as he and Bucky walked toward the gallows.

Dilda seemed composed; his face was calm. Bucky wondered if the convicted man was not more composed than he. He also noticed that not a man to whom Dilda spoke replied.

The day seemed terribly hot. Bucky's uniform was wet across the back with sweat. The cloth clung to him. As he passed one of his Grays he looked at the man, standing at rigid attention, eyes straight ahead.

Sweat was trickling down the Gray's face. Bucky hoped the sweat wouldn't get into the man's eyes. He knew how sweat burned eyes. This thought was crazy, he knew, and entirely out of context, yet it was with him.

Women and men watched Bucky and Dilda in silence. Somewhere Bucky heard sobbing. It sounded like a woman. He knew Dilda left no woman behind. During the time the man had been confined not a friend — male or female — had come to visit him.

Bucky glimpsed a townsman holding high his four-year-old son so the boy could see the man soon to be hanged. He wondered how any man could be that savage and show such stupidity. The child, in his estimation, should be home playing, not watching a hanging. The world was made of peculiar people, he thought.

He left Dilda at the gallow steps, for he'd hired another man to adjust the noose around Dilda's neck. "I just can't do it," he'd told Pauline.

Dilda looked at Bucky. "Here we go to

hell," he said, and started slowly climbing the steps.

Bucky stood below at rigid attention. His knees were rather weak, he realized; he sweated profusely, more than the heat of day demanded. Soon the noose would be adjusted around Dilda's sturdy neck.

Dilda climbed slowly, looking over the crowd. "A bunch of lousy blackhearts," he told the world in general. "Bloodthirsty ignorant animals."

Bucky, at that moment, was inclined to agree with the murderer. During his years at Yavapai he never again had to hang a man and for that he was eternally careful.

Now Dilda stood on the trapdoor. He flexed his knees and pushed his weight down as though testing the trap. The hangman asked if he wanted to wear a black mask.

Dilda laughed. "No, for sure no. Those idiots out there want to see how a man's face looks when he's dying of a broken neck. With black over my face the *locos* can't see what they came to see."

The hangman adjusted the noose. He stepped back. He gave the signal. The man below pushed the lever ahead. The trapdoor tumbled from beneath Dilda's boots.

The man crashed through the square, the big knot hitting him hard behind the left ear. Bucky heard the man's neck snap. He saw Dilda breathe deeply and heard the dying man sigh, and then Dilda was dead.

Something was wrong with the sun. It danced across the sky. Something was wrong with his knees, too. Bucky O'Neill realized he was close to fainting, and he'd never before fainted in his life.

He heard women weeping. A minister intoned a prayer beside the dead man. Suddenly Bucky O'Neill's knees stiffened, the sun settled again to its solidity. He breathed deeply and turned in best military manner.

"Prescott Grays, disperse the crowd, please. All go home or to places of business. Mr. Jones, the body is yours, sir."

The undertaker and his assistant stepped forward and began climbing the gallows. The town doctor came down. "I pronounce the prisoner officially dead, Sheriff O'Neill."

"Make your report as to time of death and manner and it will be filed in Official Records."

"You look rather pale, Bucky, if I may say so."

Bucky mopped his forehead with the back of his hand. "I don't want to ever go through this again. I honestly believe it was harder on some of us Grays than on Dilda, if that is possible."

"Those left behind sometimes suffer the most, Bucky."

CHAPTER 8

Arizona Territory was rather peaceful when William Owen O'Neill became sheriff in 1889, the bloody Pleasant Valley War finally having been brought to a conclusion by the deadly guns of Commodore Owens, sheriff of Coconino County.

Sheriff Owens was undoubtedly one of the bravest men who ever lived in the West. Singlehandedly he eliminated four gunmen of the Graham faction in one savage bloody gunfight in Holbrook, Arizona.

The gunfight took place in the old Blevins house. There Sheriff Owens fought it out with Sam Houston Blevins, Andy Cooper, Mose Roberts and John Blevins.

The gunfight raged from room to room.

131

When the Arizona wind had whipped the gunsmoke away only one of the Graham faction breathed and that was John Blevins, who was badly wounded but survived.

Sheriff Owens was, miraculously, unwounded.

Tombstone's heyday was long past. Slowly but surely it was becoming a ghost town. No longer did the Earps, the Clantons, the McLowrys and others of the gunfighter ilk walk its high streets, hands splayed over tiedown guns.

True to the engineer's prophecy, water soon flooded the big silver mines — a miner's pick one day hit an underground river's thin wall, flooding the mine with roaring water that no pumps, even those made today, could suck to the surface.

With its mines gone, Tombstone was doomed.

When Tombstone died, the last of the tough gunfighting towns followed the bloody dead path of Dodge City, Abilene and other cowtowns. Tombstone was the last of the wild mining towns just as Dodge City was the last of the hell-roaring cowtowns.

John Wesley Hardin had drawn life in Huntsville prison in Texas. The *kid* gunman was growing old and gray braiding horsehair. Ben Thompson and King Fisher, two fast gunmen, had been murdered in 1884 by a trap set by their enemies in the Vaudeville saloon in San Antonio, Texas.

Some rated Ben Thompson — the short, stove-pipe-hat gambler — as the West's fastest gunman. Thompson had outdrawn Wild Bill Hickok in wild Abilene, where Thompson and Phil Coe had run the Bullshead Saloon.

But John Wesley Hardin had also outdrawn Wild Bill. Some waited for John Wesley, the preacher's son, to match his gun against that of Ben Thompson, born in England as the son of a sailor but reared in Austin, Texas.

Now this could never be brought about. Historians would argue for eternity which of the two would have walked away alive, leaving the other a bleeding bullet-ridden lump of Texas clay.

One by one, the West's gunmen had been killed off. Doc Holliday coughed his life away somewhere in Colorado, Big

Nose Kate still following him in fistic attachment.

Buffalo Bill Cody ranched on the South Platte River. He and Ben Thompson had held a quick-draw match just before Ben's death, down in Austin.

Buffalo Bill had thrown up a can and had drawn and put five bullets in the can before it had hit the ground, missing once.

Ben Thompson had stood with his left arm rigidly extended, a poker chip lying over his thumb. At a signal he'd flipped the chip up and made his draw. He'd fired six times before the chip had hit the ground.

"You couldn't hear a silence between each shot," an Austin newspaper reporter wrote. "All six of Thompson's shots came so fast they made just one big roar! He cleanly and completely outbested Bill Cody!"

The Earps had fled Tombstone, a federal charge against Wyatt, who never drew a cent as a Tombstone lawman, according to extant Tombstone city records. Nobody knew where Earp was hiding out.

Arizona Territory longed to become a

State. Bucky O'Neill worked for this status through editorials in his *Hoofs and Horns*. Arizona sent orators East to try to convince new settlers to move to the Territory for with enough population the Territory would be bound to become a state.

An Arizona orator finished a lengthy diatribe in New York City, stressing all the favorable points his territory possessed. He leveled his forefinger at his audience.

"Arizona needs but two things," he thundered. "Plenty of water and good neighbors!"

Somebody in the front row said, "Mister, that's all they need in Hell, also!"

Rails had been laid by the Southern Pacific into Phoenix and then down to Tucson and Tombstone and Douglas and so out of the Territory into New Mexico.

The Santa Fe ran north of Prescott through Ashfork but Prescott had no railroad — another thing that *Hoofs and Horns* fought for editorially.

Arizona was fast becoming a quiet area. Apaches were on reservations and seldom if ever broke the limits of those reservations. Prescott now had a telegraph station, the wire being strung down from the Santa Fe Railroad's wires at Ashfork, some fifty miles straight north on the high windswept Arizona plains.

A wire also ran up from Southern Pacific poles in Phoenix. Prescott now had communication with the outside world but all passengers and freight still had to arrive and depart through stagecoach and freighting wagons.

Once again, Sheriff William Owen O'Neill had trouble with the Texas cowboys, the same old Hashknife outfit that had plagued Marshal Garfias in Phoenix some eight years or so before.

Hashknife ran longhorns on the northeast section of Sheriff O'Neill's bailiwick, and although they left Prescott alone, that was because Prescott was just a small town and was far to the west of the beaten path to bigger Phoenix.

Hashknife had caused almost all the range trouble in northern Arizona since the arrogant Texas spread had dumped around fifty thousand head of wild Texas longhorns over the Mogollon Rim down into the Tonto Basin and other scattered

Arizona northeastern points.

Sheepmen had instantly risen up in arms and the war had been savage and long, but most of it had taken place far west of Bucky's country — and that had been the concern of Sheriff Commodore Owens.

On one cold, windy snow-laden night in March of 1889 four masked men wearing big Stetsons and cowboy garb had halted and stuck up a Santa Fe train heading west in the far northeast section of Bucky's domain.

The cowboys looted passengers of jewelry, money and other valuables and then lifted a nice sum of money from the express car. The holdup occurred where Santa Fe rails crossed a deep canyon in the Little Colorado River called Canon Diablo — the Devil's Canyon.

After the robbery the passenger train was allowed to resume its trip west to Los Angeles, pushing its iron nose into the chilly wind that tore across the high plateau — a bone-cutting cold wind that carried hard wisps of freezing snow.

Morning of March 22 — the morning after the holdup — dawned icily cold in the pines of Prescott, the mountains bearing crowns of snow and the pine trees coated in ice. Bucky's breath had hung like a white cloud in front of him that morning when, bundled in sheepskin coat and muskrat-skin cap, he'd opened his office and stamped the snow from his overshoes.

The court house janitor had a good fire going in Bucky's potbellied cast iron coal heater and Bucky was warming his back when the telegraph operator burst in without knocking, his face red and flushed from the cold wind.

"Sheriff O'Neill — This wire — It just now came in from the Santa Fe — in Los Angeles —"

Bucky read the rather lengthy telegram, his youthful face hardening. Then, anger assailed him. The holdup had taken place at eleven last night. It was now ten after nine the next morning.

More than ten hours had elapsed since the four, apparently cowboys, had held up the Santa Fe train. Why hadn't the stupid railroad officials wired him right after the holdup?

Surely the conductor of the train had called in from the next depot west to report the robbery? Railroad officials should have then called his office and he'd have been immediately on the trail.

By now the outlaws had a good ten hour start. Bucky walked to the big wall map showing the entire Territory. He laid a yardstick across the map, pointing the ruler northeast.

He put the end of the yardstick on Prescott and then noted where *Canon Diablo* came on the stick. He then looked at the map's scale of miles and figured it was, as the crow flew, about eighty-five or ninety miles to the scene of the stickup.

The telegram said that three Santa Fe special agents would be awaiting him in Flagstaff at the Santa Fe depot. Flagstaff was about sixty-five miles northeast in the high pines.

He'd have to ride to Flagstaff on horseback. Within an hour Sheriff William Owen O'Neill rode out of Prescott astraddle his favorite and toughest saddler, a line-backed mouse-colored buckskin gelding he'd named Sandy. Sandy was a four-year-old and at the peak of his endurance and ability.

Sandy's dam had been the sorrel mare

who'd fallen with Bucky the time he'd broken his arm in the forest. Sandy's sire had been a range buckskin stud noted for his toughness on the trail.

From his mother Sandy had inherited a certain daintiness and a fast running-walk that could cover miles and miles a day. From his range horse sire he'd got a toughness that fitted him to any trail be it up mountain or down.

Bucky — and Sandy — didn't know it but the morning they left Prescott, they, the man and horse, began what was to become perhaps the longest legal manhunt ever performed on horseback. Neither did the two know that this ride would again bring the name of Bucky O'Neill back into household use throughout the United States.

Bucky rode north to Ashfork, reaching that little railroad town at dark, his horse was tired and he himself wind-hammered and cold. It was even chillier in Ashfork than in Prescott for Ashfork was on the level plains and high mountains and pines somewhat protected Prescott.

He loaded Sandy into a box car where the bronc had oats and hay and water and

Bucky ate cold sandwiches washed down with cold water as the freight pulled slowly east toward Flagstaff, which was reached at early dawn, the boxcar being shunted onto a siding, the rest of the freight train pulling on east.

Here the three Santa Fe special agents had their horses, packs and gear waiting. Bucky knew each man well.

Cal Holton was a tall, middle-aged man, tough as rawhide. Equally durable and trustworthy were squat Jim Black and lanky slow-speaking Ed St. Clair.

A loading gate was put up to the door of Bucky's boxcar and the three horses were led inside, Sandy snorting at them and pawing the floor, rested again and ready for the trail.

A steam locomotive was hooked onto the boxcar which began to roll rapidly east toward *Canon Diablo,* the locomotive picking up speed and whipping the lone boxcar around curves.

"Now we're moving," Bucky told Ed St. Clair.

"They got a long start on us," St. Clair said. "The sign reads like Hashknife, although a man can't be sure at this stage of the game."

The boxcar was very cold, the breath of the horses and men standing out in whiteness. Bucky tugged his sheepskin's high collar up tighter. "And they've only got a thirty hour start," he said, grinning at his own jest.

"Why in the hell couldn't they rob that train during the summertime, when it was warm?" Cal Holton said.

Dawn was bright when finally the boxcar was shunted onto a siding on the east lip of *Canon Diablo*. Again the ramp was put into place and the horses led down, the mounts bracing steel-shod hoofs against the pull of gravity, snorting and dancing in their new environment.

Here on the eastern plains the wind howled hungrily, its icy fingers cutting even through Bucky's thick sheepskin coat and angora chaps.

Bucky walked to the lip of *Canon Diablo* and gazed into its snow-scattered depths where only scraggly juniper and mesquite trees grew, their roots clinging onto the canyon's rocky slope.

The high bridge stretched across the canyon, a ribbon of steel and crossties held up by high steel girders anchored in concrete in the abyss below. You could see the Little Colorado River, almost frozen over, as it pushed its narrow way northwest to its final junction with the Colorado River in the Grand Canyon.

"They might not have pulled out," Bucky said. "They might be in the vicinity."

"Let's hope they are," Jim Black said.

Cal Holton said, "I doubt that. I wish we had some good descriptions to run on. Those passengers were so scared of those guns they got things all mixed up and we've not got much to go on, men."

The railroad had a caretaker who watched the bridge. He lived in a log house on the east bank of the canyon. He told the four manhunters a few things they didn't already know.

Somebody had brought him to his door by knocking last night at ten. He had answered. Four men had jumped him. They'd borne him down, blindfolded him, then had gagged him and tied him hand and foot.

Bucky and his men and the old watchman were drinking coffee from the

143

black pot on the old watchman's red hot heater. Bucky noticed that the old man's hand trembled.

Was the trembling caused by fear of last night's grisly happenings or old age? Bucky was inclined to think fear prompted the trembling.

A pile of railroad crossties were piled behind the watchman's shack. The four bandits had piled some ties across the track just where the rails left the bridge and ran onto hard earth again.

Of course the passenger train moved slowly across the high, dangerous wooden bridge. The four had used the watchman's red kerosene lantern to flag the train to a stop.

"You got any idea who they were?" Bucky asked.

The old watchman surprised all by blandly saying, "Sure I know who they were. They're the four Hashknife cowboys winterin' in the Canyon down below where Clear Crick comes into the Little Colorado!"

Bucky and Ed St. Clair exchanged surprised glances. "How do you know these four were those four Hashknife men?"

"Sure, they were masked. They all wore long sheepskin coats and when they talked they never called each other by name but I know their voices and their builds."

"You know their names?" Bucky knew that this was undoubtedly a valuable bit of information.

"Dan Harvick is cabin boss. Them Hashknife cowboys are at that cabin to turn back Hashknife cows that want to drift with the storms. Most storms here come from the northwest and the cattle tend to drift southeast and —"

"Please," Bucky said. "Harvick is one. Who are the other three?"

"Harvick's about thirty. Short, heavy-set. Tough gent in a rough and tumble. They say he can use his gun, too. The other three?"

"Yes," Bucky patiently said. "The names of the others."

"Bill Stiron's one. Lanky stringbean guy about twenty-five. John Halford is a small gink. Then there's J. J. Smith."

The oldster paused. Evidently he liked being the center of attention. Finally Bucky asked, "What about J. J. Smith?"

"He's got a bad scar. I forget which cheek it's on. Got in a big fight with some Mexican sheepherders last year over in Holbrook in a saloon. Mexes don't fight with guns. They use steel. An' afore Smith could kill the Mex the *senora* son cut up J. J. rather bad."

Bucky spoke to his men. "You boys know any of these Texans this gentleman has just mentioned?"

Cal Holton had had J. J. Smith pointed out to him a few times on his travels up and down this section of the Santa Fe track doing his police duties. "This gentleman is right, Bucky. Smith's cut up pretty bad. I'd know him anywhere just by his scar."

Ed St. Clair and Jim Black knew none of the Texans. Bucky turned his attention again to the coffee pot and the watchman. "Which way did they leave after the robbery?"

"They went south. The engineer freed me. I got my lantern and looked for tracks before the wind blowed them away or snow covered them and they went south — all four horses of them."

Bucky scowled. He rubbed his whiskery

jaw. Going south didn't make sense for south lay the Fort Apache Indian Reservation.

Although Geronimo had been captured in 1886 and the Apaches were presumably on rather good terms with the whites on military paper Bucky knew that the Apaches still hated the *paleface.*

Logic then told him the robbers wouldn't have to ride across Fort Apache Reservation. They could swing east and follow the north boundary of the reservation into New Mexico Territory and be lost in the heavy timber around Silver City — timber through which he'd ridden ten years ago on his burro when he'd entered Arizona Territory.

Or they could follow the northern boundary of the reservation to the west, drop down the Mogollon Rim into the Tonto, then go on to Phoenix or miss Phoenix and drift south down the Gila to Gila Bend. There they could leave the Gila and ride straight south into *Sonora* state in old Mexico.

According to the oldster, the Clear Creek cabin where the four Texans had been stationed was a good thirty miles southeast — a long ride but one Bucky knew they'd have to make, for the men might have been foolish enough to think they'd not been recognized and might have returned to their winter quarters.

"To saddles, men," Bucky O'Neill ordered.

CHAPTER 9

Bucky and his men mounted and rode due south, the four manhunters spread out about a hundred yards apart. Wind howled and bent knee-high gray sagebrush and willows in draws were covered with dirty snow.

The hard wind of last night and today had swept the sandy soil clean of tracks except in *arroyos* and coulees, and not even an Apache brave could trail a man on this soil. There simply were no tracks, that was all.

Four miles south of the railroad was a long draw running crosscurrents to the wind and it was in this that sharp-eyed Cal Holton found the tracks of the four mounted Texans.

"Shod horses, men. Four of them, too. Tracks run into that little coulee over yonderly, looks like," the railroad special agent said.

Shod horses meant these were saddlehorses, not rangehorses. When a saddlehorse was sent out to range his shoes were pulled off him so he'd get in no trouble getting hung up on wire fences and such.

The four followed the trail into the small coulee, their broncs sliding in shale against gravity and here, to their surprise, they found a sheltered sandy area whose surface was punctured by high heel riding boots — cowboy boots, even with an occasional scar in the sand made by trailing spur rowels.

Ed St. Clair picked up a cheap gold-plated earring, the kind today they call costume jewelry. "They've split their loot here. They've throwed this away as worthless, I suppose. Then they've mounted and gone which way, men?"

"Looks like the tracks run toward the south down this gully," Bucky said. "Let's follow them and see what's what?"

The tracks ran straight south for about a hundred yards and then to everybody's surprise circled out of the coulee and turned east to follow the shale toe of a rimrock ledge.

Bucky scowled. "Surely they aren't heading for their Clear Creek camp after throwing away that earring where anybody trailing could find it. They're not that stupid, are they?"

Cal Holton said, "I wish I knew if that Clear Creek camp was empty or had four Texans in it. Sure'd be a long cold ride over there. And if we found the cabin empty we'd have wasted about two days' time and we're late as it is."

"Thank the railroad officials for that," Bucky said drily.

The four manhunters followed under the rimrock, now losing the tracks, now finding them again. Five miles ticked past and then suddenly the tracks left the coulee and headed up a canyon that ran north to meet the Little Colorado River a few miles above the Santa Fe railroad bridge where the robbery had occurred.

Jim Black said, "We've rid in about a circle, men. They've led us south and then circled and now they're headin' north."

"That makes sense," Cal Holton said. "North a few hundred miles or so is Utah and the badlands where the Wild Bunch and those gents hang out. That's a god-awful lonesome country up there and those Mormons don't like non-Mormons pokin' in their noses."

Bucky pulled in Sandy. The others momentarily rested their broncs also. Bucky looked north across endless, limitless space. Gray sagebrush and cut coulees and deer and antelope and a few drifting cowboys and finally the Grand Canyon of the Colorado as the big river plunged downward toward the Gulf of California from its starting point high in the northern Rockies.

He didn't know this country. A few questions told him his fellow manhunters had never ridden across southern Utah, either.

The wind was very, very cold. They were at a high altitude. They had only the grub they packed in saddlebags but of course they had rifles and could live off the land — antelope, deer, sagehens, grouse and if things got too tough, there was always the long-eared jackrabbit.

Bucky spoke to Jim Black. "We're riding north. Jim, ride back and get a wire out to the railroad officials in Los Angeles that we're on the trail and pushing toward Utah. Get a wire to my office in Prescott, too. It might be some time until we come back."

Jim Black turned his bronc southeast. "Okay, Bucky." He left at a high lope, the wind whipping his bronc's tail between the horse's hind legs.

Those wires were the last the world heard of Bucky O'Neill and his three-man posse for some time, for where they rode there were no telegraph lines or railroads or mail service.

They turned northwest into a wilderness that today is just about as savage and relentless as it then was.

They traversed the north-south limits of what today is the immense Navajo Indian Reservation, a rugged and heartless desert land of torrid summer heat and howling winter cold that even today is marked by only two roads that meet at Moenkopi, one coming down from Utah and the other coming in from what today is the State of New Mexico.

Heads down against the icy northwest wind, they rode across the great Painted

Desert, one of the world's most isolated and lonesome stretches. "And most people imagine a desert as always being boiling hot," Bucky O'Neill said through cold blue lips.

They trailed down the Little Colorado to what today is called Wupatki National Monument, roughly forty-odd miles from *Canon Diablo*. They had to conserve horseflesh and, at the same time, keep careful watch over what horses they had, so they took turns standing nightguard for two hours each, the others catching fitful sleep back in the Wupatki ruins — the cliff dwellings of a race of men that long ago had ceased to walk the lonely earth.

Ed St. Clair rubbed his whiskery jaw. "There must be a better way to make a living for the woman and kids," he said jokingly.

Bucky smiled. "What other would it be? We're free and we pay no taxes. We can come and go where we want within limits of a benevolent law. We can hunt and fish when we care to."

Jim Black said, "We'd need water to fish in. There isn't much water here — just a few springs that pack enough for man and beast."

"That's all a person needs," Cal Holton said.

They pushed down the Little Colorado again, the stream growing wider as side creeks came in. Now Gray Mountain was to their left across the tumbling wilderness.

Occasionally they glimpsed the hogans of the Navajos and these they avoided, for legally they had no right to ride on reservation soil — they had no permission from the Navajo headmen.

Toward noon they came around a bend in the Painted Desert country and blundered on a Navajo boy and his sister herding long-haired goats at the base of the *mesa*.

The children took one look at the whitemen, ran for their ponies and galloped away west, apparently forgetting their goats, which stood and looked at the four horsemen, their mouths open as they bleated what apparently was a greeting.

Bucky said, "They'll get on some high ridge and watch and when we are gone they'll come back again. Those angora goats there would make good chaps to cover a man's legs against this cold wind."

"I'd like a pair made out of that black and white nanny there," Jim Black said.

"Down in middle Texas a few years back King Fisher jumped a circus wagon and shot the tiger and had chaps made of that cat's skin," Ed St. Clair said. "Now that King got his along with Ben Thompson, I wonder where those chaps went to."

"Probably some madame in some cathouse has them hanging on her wall," Cal Holton said. "King was a great one to patronize the females, I understand."

Talk, just idle talk, nothing more. But it passed the time and bound them together as they inched northwest across this immensity, not even as big as ants cross a ballroom's enormous floor.

They spent that night at what is now Cameron, Arizona, and here in this pioneer settlement they learned that the four Texans they sought had been sighted to the far east, heading north.

"Cowboy for the Diamon' Bar saw them. He rode after them a ways, wantin' to know what they was doin' on his spread's graze, because there's been a heap of cow-stealin' goin' on ag'in Diamon' Bar, you know.''

The four had shot back at the cowboy, halting his bronc in its tracks. The cowboy had wanted nothing to do with this quartet of lone wolves.

Bucky and his men slept that night in the haymow of a small-time rancher's barn after they'd all promised not to smoke. ''The four are heading for Lee's Ferry,'' he told his men.

''Only place they could go,'' Ed St. Clair said. ''Only place a man can cross the Colorado in miles and miles, I've heard.''

''They're headin' for Utah and the Wild Bunch country,'' Cal Holton said. ''They'll be hard to find there because somebody's told me that that country is all rough with painted badlands and hanging natural bridges.''

''Can't be any rougher than that we put behind us the last few days,'' Jim Black said. ''I got to smoke. I'll go downstairs, men.'' And he began climbing down the haymow ladder.

Bucky left word next morning with the

rancher that the rancher try to get word out that he and his posse had moved through heading for Utah, the four Hashknife holdup men riding ahead.

Sandy, tough as he was, held up better than the other cayuses, who lacked Sandy's conditioning and blood. They'd tried to get new mounts at the rancher's spread but he had only makeshift cayuses that even when fresh were not the horses that Sandy and the others were even if tired.

Lee's Ferry on the Colorado was now about seventy miles straight north, so at this point they left the Little Colorado, which flowed northwest to its meeting with the big Colorado in the Grand Canyon.

They followed Moenkopi Wash for about eight miles, then left it where it angled almost directly east. They had to cross endless miles of Painted Desert now as they rode toward Lee's Ferry on the Colorado.

That night they pitched camp in a gap in the badlands. They'd shot a buck deer and they skinned out his hind quarters and cut steaks which they fried in a pan Bucky had in his pack tied behind his saddle.

Next morning they again dined on the deer, having hung the quarter high in a smoketree, but coyotes and other predators had made deep inroads into the remainder of the deer which had been left where he'd fallen.

They were now about forty miles south of Lee's Ferry. Rough country lay ahead but you didn't put your leg-tired bronc up steep slopes; you followed coulees and only climbed ridges when forced to. They camped that night at Bitter Springs, some twelve miles below the ferry.

"Sure, I saw four riders headin' north," a sheepman said in broken English, for he was a Basque recently imported to herd sheep for very cheap wages. "They were goin' north toward Lee's Ferry."

"Can you describe them?" Bucky asked.

"What does *describe* mean?"

Bucky shrugged and walked away. Next forenoon they rode down the rough wagon-trail leading to Lee's Ferry, the only crossing place on the Colorado for a hundred miles or so up or down the river.

Were the four Texans to go into Utah

over this route they'd have to cross at Lee's Ferry, therefore the ferryman should know if they had or hadn't. Sandy moved down the trail, braced against the slope, the other three riders following.

Once a horse dislodged a small rock. The rock rolled off the lip of the road and fell hundreds of feet below, its sound finally ringing back. Bucky looked at his left. There was a solid stone wall.

Dynamite, picks and shovels had laboriously made this descent wide enough for a wagon to move downward.

As they descended the rising opposite lip of the Grand Canyon cut off the wind. Bucky was glad for that. With the wind gone the sun was almost warm on this late March day.

He'd not been warmed by the sun for months now. He and his posse had ridden heads-down against the wind all the distance from faraway *Canon Diablo*.

He noticed that the ferry was on the north bank of the river. That meant the ferryman had used his low flat-bottomed boat to move passengers to the opposite shore the last time the boat was used.

Bucky figured the ferryman slept on

whichever bank of the Colorado he happened to land for the night, for it appeared he had two shacks, one on either side. Both shacks appeared to have been lived in, for the one on the far side had a plume of smoke rising from the stovepipe chimney.

This south side of the ferry consisted of a sandbar with a bit of grass, and Bucky judged it to be about ten acres, no more. He dismounted and pulled the bell rope, bringing the ferryman from his shack across the river.

The man waved and got into his boat, the long steel pole pushing the ferry from its mooring, the current catching the boat and drifting it to the dock where the posse waited.

The ferryman was an aged individual with tobacco brown running down his short gray beard. "Wanna cross, cowboys?"

"That's why we're here," Bucky said. "Four other cowboys are riding ahead of us. We haven't been able to catch them."

Holton, Black and St. Clair remained silent, letting Bucky do the questioning. For one moment, all hung in suspense, for the ferryman bit off a fresh chew, tobacco-black teeth cutting his plug of Horseshoe.

Finally, the teeth had cut loose what the mouth wanted, and the back teeth then began masticating. Only then did the ferryman say, "They crossed late last night, cowboys."

Bucky described the four Hashknife riders as well as he could remember the old railroad watchman's description. "That's the four," the ferryman said. "Lead your broncs onto the platform and across we go. A buck a horse and rider, so four bucks in all."

Bucky nodded. "Okay with me."

"Payable in advance, cowboy."

Bucky looked at the man. "Don't you trust me, man? Usually a man pays after a service is rendered and not before."

"Pay me now or on this side of the river you stay unless you gun me down," the skinny man savagely said. "Them four crossed last night an' never paid a cent. They told me to kiss my sitter and they rode off with me in front of one of them, hollerin' like hell."

Bucky almost grinned but held it in

time. "They didn't want to leave you behind and pick them off with your rifle, huh?"

"That's the deal, men. They set me down out in the rough country and I had to leg it about a mile into camp."

Bucky dug up four silver dollars. "Here's your pay, friend. From what I've heard Apaches had raided this crossing once or twice. How come you don't have a dog?"

"Dogs no count against Injuns. They slit his throat an' he's done. Me, I got them guinea hens you see scratchin' along the river bank. Got 'em on both sides. Better'n any dog made."

Bucky had heard that ranchers had guinea hens to warn them of Indian attacks for a guinea roosts high in a tree and nothing escapes his ears or eyes. He'll cackle during the night even if a light only goes on in the ranchhouse.

The posse pulled its leg-weary horses onto the leading ramp and then onto the barge, the horses not protesting much because of weariness. Bucky asked if the ferryman could rent them fresh horses for they'd be coming back this way in a short time.

The man shook his head. "That's another thing those bastards last night did — they stole four of my top saddlestock and left their ol' Hashknife stock behin'. That's why I ain't got no hosses to rent you four boys."

Bucky's heart sank. Freshly mounted, the four holdup men could rapidly leave this posse in its dust. His depression soon lifted, though. His few months as sheriff had taught him that patience and not rashness usually won out in the end.

The Hashknife riders had crossed the Colorado about midnight, the old man judged, but he wasn't sure — his watch had dropped from his pocket about eight years ago and nobody'd ever come along that could repair it.

Ed St. Clair winked at Bucky without the ferryman seeing it. "Odd Mack and the boys never waited for us. They must be in Utah by now. How far is it to the Utah line, ferryman?"

"About twelve, thirteen miles. They never said a word about you boys behin' 'em. They never tol' me where they were goin' in Utah, either."

"What's the closest town to here in Utah?" Bucky asked.

His reasoning was that the Hashknife men would hit for the closest source of supplies for undoubtedly their larder would be running low. And, naturally, men gravitated toward other men and most men immediately went to the closest town or city.

"Ain't no doggone town at all up the river until you get to Hite, an' that's a good hundred miles away. I ain't never been but to Hite in Utah. When I go to town it's down to Flagstaff."

The ferryman's squaw fed them. Bucky cradled his hands around a good cup of coffee, for a change. Luck was with him at this point for waiting to cross south came a young couple with three children in a wagon pulled by two black mules.

The couple had come down from Kanab, Utah, almost ninety miles directly east, a town smack on the Arizona-Utah border. They were moving to Flagstaff where the husband had been promised work as a logger.

They'd been on the road three days. They'd not met four riders heading toward

Kanab, the man related. "Only met one buggy in all the distance and that was a rancher going into Kanab for supplies."

The young wife said, "I rode horseback most of the way because I like to ride the hills and look around and I only saw one person outside of my family and that rancher, and he was an Indian herding sheep way off in the distance."

Ed St. Clair again winked secretly at Bucky. "Seems to me the boys said they'd meet us straight north of this ferry."

Bucky caught the cue. "What town is the closest up north?" he asked the young husband.

"Oh, that's Cannonville," the man answered without a moment of hesitation. "About sixty, seventy miles north. You hit the Paria river right here at the ferry and follow it north."

"That's where they said they'd meet us," Bucky said. "I remember now. Cannonville."

"Ain't been nobody down from Cannonville for a long, long time," the ferryman said, "so I can't tell you if nobody met your friends goin' north or not. Another deer steak, cowboy?"

Bucky got the young man to one side and told him his identity, for he wanted the man to notify Pauline in Prescott that her husband was safe at Lee's Ferry along with Black, Holton and St. Clair.

"Wire the court house in Prescott. My undersheriff will accept the wire collect. How many days do you figure it will take you to get to Flagstaff?"

Within the hour, Bucky and his manhunters rode north, this time leaving the Colorado River behind, following one of its biggest tributaries, the Paria, which angled almost due north across the Arizona-Utah border from its source in the high Paunsaugunt Plateau, today known as Bryce Canyon National Park, located in southcentral Utah.

Two hours later Bucky suddenly laughed. "What's so comical?" Ed St. Clair asked.

"By now we must be in Utah and neither of us has a bit of jurisdiction outside of Arizona Territory!"

Jim Black shrugged. "Ed an' Cal an' me's hired to protect Santa Fe property. Me, I ain't got no love for any railroad, big or small — they gobble up too much property when they lay rails because Uncle Sam gives them so much land on either side of the right-of-ways to induce them to lay rails."

Bucky nodded. He'd many times thought the same.

"But if a man hires me to work for him he buys my time and part of my life," Jim Black continued, "an' my job is to give him his money's worth in labor. And if one bunch robbed the Santa Fe and got off with it there'd be an open season on robbing Santa Fe trains."

"The same goes for me," Bucky said. "If I don't catch these train robbers the fact that they held up a train in Yavapai County and got away with it would be an open invitation for others to rob in my county."

"We're all getting too serious," Ed St. Clair said. "I glimpsed a young buck jump into those willows over to the left. We need meat for this evening, huh?"

"Deer are all over the place," Cal Holton said. "Shoot one closer to camp. We won't have to pack him so far then."

"That sounds logical," Ed St. Clair said.

Cal Holton looked about him. They were on the west bank of the Paria, having forded the stream a few miles back in the ripples. He pointed toward the toe of the western hills, some half mile away.

"A man could build his ranchhouse there with corrals on the slant where the drainage would be good. He could dam this river and shoot water into canals and irrigate during dry summers and live like a king with alfalfa to his chin."

"Quit daydreaming," Bucky said jokingly.

CHAPTER 10

Bucky and his posse rode into Cannonville at four the next afternoon, having passed the night in a brush camp along the murmuring Paria. Cannonville consisted of a bunch of frame buildings strung out along the river's cottonwood trees, its main street consisting of one graveled block flanked by wooden buildings, most of them badly in need of paint.

Apparently all the town's population — men, women, children and babies — were on the gravel walks staring at Bucky and his three men, with Bucky noticing immediately the town held few children — which told him the population consisted mostly of men.

The young man back at Lee's Ferry had told Bucky that Cannonville men ran cattle back in the hills and panned a little gold from the Paria.

He'd also told Bucky that this southern section of Utah was almost all Mormon and because the Mormons had been so persecuted by the government they were very, very leery of strangers. This, to Bucky, was only natural.

Thus Bucky and his men could have been riding between two ranks of deadly enemies for nobody spoke to them or lifted a hand in greeting. Despite the absence of short-guns on hips and rifles in hands, Bucky had a cold feeling along his spine.

A stolid, heavy-set grayhaired man stood on the corner, watching them advance through heavily-lidded blue eyes. Something about his patriarchal air made Bucky believe him to be the town leader. Accordingly he drew rein before the old man, Holton and Black and St. Clair also drawing in.

"Are you the town mayor?" Bucky politely asked.

The gray silky beard nodded. The pale blue eyes evaluated Bucky, but the thick lips made no movement.

Patiently, Bucky repeated his question.

This time he received the slow reply of, "Yes, I'm what could be called the mayor, if this town had one." He gave his name. "And who are you four strangers and what is your mission here?"

Bucky had met quite a few Mormons in Arizona and had discovered that when a Mormon gave you his word that word was always — yes, always — good, so he decided to be honest with this man.

He then told the patriarch the names of his men and his station and name and he told all about the Santa Fe robbery and how he and these Santa Fe special agents had trailed the four robbers north.

The old man nodded. He didn't offer his hand; he kept silent, eyes on Bucky.

Bucky asked, "Have you seen our four robbers ride through here, or near here?"

Finally, the thick lips said, "No, only you four strangers."

"I accept that," Bucky said.

Without a word, the old man wheeled in military fashion and entered a building which carried the faded legend: GENERAL STORE. It was as though his leaving had been an order for all others to hurriedly desert the street, and within a few moments Bucky and his men sat alone, the sidewalks empty of people.

Ed St. Clair shoved back his hat. "We sure didn't learn much there. You suppose he told the truth, Bucky?"

"I think so. They're honest people. Government isn't persecuting them for anything but having a few wives too many, nothing more."

"We could search every building and stable in town," Cal Holton said. "Wouldn't take long. There aren't many of such."

"Not that," Bucky quickly said. "Their religion doesn't want them to pack six-shooters or rifles when in peace but they'll sure fight when pushed, and nobody knows that better than Hashknife's Texans."

All knew what Bucky referred to. Hashknife had thrown its thousands of head of cattle onto land grazed by the sheep of Mormon settlers. Hashknife had discovered that Mormons, although easy-going on the surface, were hell-on-boots when angered.

Bucky didn't know how many Hashknife men Mormons had wounded or killed, or vice-versa — but he did know that Sheriff Commodore Owens had had his hands full with Mormons and Texans over in the northeast corner of Arizona Territory.

Bucky had emphasized that the four he searched for were Hashknife riders, and when he'd said that he'd been sure the gray eyes of the Mormon elder had for once shown a bit of life.

Were Hashknife riders to fall into the hands of these Mormons, life would become rough for Hashknife, Bucky guessed. Mormons were closely related by blood through multiple marriages. Undoubtedly some of Cannonville's people had relatives that had been fighting or were fighting Hashknife now down in Arizona.

There was a public livery-barn and a sort of cafe in Cannonville and Sandy and his three companions dined in the barn and Bucky and his three in the cafe, where the home-cooking was excellent.

While Bucky was eating, the graybearded elder entered and took a stool and ordered pie and water for the cafe had no beverages — not even tea and coffee — for to drink such drinks was contrary to Mormon beliefs.

When finished Bucky paid at the counter and he said softly to the elder, "There's fifty dollars each bounty on those four men, sir."

The elder apparently never heard. He didn't nod or look up. Bucky and his men rode out without a soul on the street watching but Bucky bet many a window curtain was moved slightly to one side.

"What'd you tell grandpa?" Cal Holton asked Bucky.

Bucky told him. Ed St. Clair laughed. "We pay a two hundred buck reward and we'd be eating wild onions with the sagehens, Bucky."

Bucky grinned. "We wouldn't pay it. Those Hashknife outlaws would."

Ed St. Clair grinned. "Never thought of that. Wonder how many thousand they got off with."

Nobody knew, of course. Railroad officials hadn't had time to determine the monetary loss when Bucky and the special agents had gone to work.

"Well, they sure got more than two hundred bucks," Cal Holton said, "and they haven't had a chance to spend a cent since leaving *Canon Diablo*. I haven't seen a saloon on the way up."

"And there'll be none in this section of Utah," Bucky said, "because Mormons don't drink alcohol."

"I can't see why hard drinking men would enter this area," Jim Black put in.

"Where else could they escape to?" Cal Holton asked. "They go south and they'd run into Arizona law. I'd say they were heading still further north to get on a railroad somewhere. Some place like Provo or Salt Lake City, I'd judge."

"I think you're right," Bucky said. "I gave that young fellow back at Lee's Ferry a note telling railroad officials to keep close watch on passengers boarding trains in Utah."

"Good idea," Ed St. Clair said. "Those guys have gone through here or are located somewhere in this valley. Where do we head for now, sheriff?"

"There's a town called Paria ten miles up the river. Let's inquire there and spend the night there."

Nobody had shaved since starting out, which was at least a week or ten days back — none had kept accurate track of days, although the rest of the United States had, for newspapers throughout the nation carried stories of the sheriff who'd plunged into the wilderness with three railroad special agents to trace down and capture or kill four train robbers.

Bucky and Cal Holton worked the timbered country on the west bank of the river and Ed St. Clair and Jim Black worked the east side but when they met at Paria each had seen only a few drifting Navajo Indians that had plainly jumped their Arizona reservation.

Paria consisted of one General Store which had a cafe and rooms for rent overhead. The storekeeper had seen no strangers for months except Bucky and his men. Bucky hired rooms for the night, a feeling of fear in him. He and his men might have ridden north from Lee's Ferry on a cold trail.

That night the four slept on featherticks, their tired horses in a hired pasture high with wild bear-grass. Next morning the quartet was eating ham and eggs and wishing they had some coffee when a young man burst into view, whipping his pinto mare down the hind legs for more speed.

He hit the ground on the run, bootheels digging. Bucky had seen the youth down in Cannonville so he'd hurried out, Ed St. Clair at his spurs and Jim Black following Ed, with Cal Holton taking up the rear.

"Mr. O'Neill, Cannonville has captured your outlaws. They rode into town early this morning, sheriff!"

Bucky could only stare in amazement for a long moment. He and his men had ridden past their quarry? He looked at the stunned whiskery faces of his three companions.

"They took a day off to rest their horses," Ed St. Clair said. "They were camped back somewhere in the brush when we rode north. We're danged lucky they never seen us or they'd have wheeled off west or east or maybe drifted back south again."

"Where are the men now?" Bucky spoke to the excited youth.

"They're under heavy guard in the strongest building Cannonville's got. We're waitin' for you to pay us all the two hundred bucks, Sheriff O'Neill."

Bucky paid for the meals and the night lodging and soon he and his men were in saddle, riding fast south with the youth.

The boy shouted information above the pounding of hurrying hoofs. Two outlaws had ridden in first, one being a big man with a huge scar on his face, which had to be J. J. Smith, Bucky figured.

The other rider had been a short, strong-shouldered man whom Bucky picked to be Dan Harvick, judging from the old railroad watchman's description.

The two had asked where the saloon was but of course Cannonville had no saloon. They'd then gone to the cafe to eat, and while eating, armed citizens had surrounded them and caught them by surprise and made them captives.

The Cannonville citizens didn't lead the train-robbers' horses from the street but left them there as decoy for the other two robbers, whom they felt sure would follow.

"They all led extra horses," the youth said. "One of the extra cayuses has got a big pack on him."

Bucky hoped that pack held train-robbery money. If it didn't he and his friends might have a hard time meeting a two hundred dollar account. And if this two hundred wasn't paid, the citizens of Cannonville might incarcerate one Bucky O'Neill and three Santa Fe railroad special agents and put four train-robbers free, for all Cannonville wanted was the two hundred dollars, nothing more.

Two hours later Bill Stiron and John Halford had ridden into Cannonville and upon seeing the horses of Smith and Harvick tied before the cafe they'd swung down into the cold steel of rifles and shortguns in the hands of Mormons who had miraculously appeared around corners and from behind them across the street.

"Well, we got them," Ed St. Clair said.

"You'll have to pay the two hundred before you take them out of Cannonville," the youth said. "If you don't maybe you'll go to jail for a while while the others are turned loose, huh?"

"Such terrible talk," Jim Black joked. But was it a joke?

When the five horsemen plunged into the center of Cannonville the town was in an uproar. The graybeard patriarch, fuming with anger and disappointment, now was only too eager to pant the story to Bucky.

"They've done escaped us," he mourned, eyes watery and sad.

Strangely, Bucky felt a moment of almost elation. Now they'd not have to worry about paying two hundred dollars! Then the realization struck him with full force.

He had a sudden idea. He suddenly felt sure the bandits had bought themselves out of this mess. "They ride out on their horses?" he demanded.

"They did, sir."

"They lead their other horses — their extra broncs — with them?"

"That they did," the graybeard said.

Bucky scowled, glancing at Ed St. Clair, whose gray eyes had gone hard and small. Jim Black flanked Ed on Ed's right, and his lips were tight and, on Ed's left, Cal Holton's eyes were dangerous and mean. Evidently each of them had the same suspicions that plagued Bucky at this moment.

"Which way'd they go?" Bucky asked.

Graybeard shrugged but a young woman said angrily, "They went west,

Mister O'Neill.'' Graybeard sent her a hard glance that plainly told her to keep her mouth shut but she said, angrily, "To hell with you, Elder Nothing,'' and strode away, back straight in anger.

"You shall pay in the Hereafter for this,'' the elder called to her.

"If there is such a crazy thing,'' the woman said, entering a house and going out of sight.

"Nothing we can do here,'' Bucky said.

Ed St. Clair said, "I'd like to see where the bandits were held and how they escaped, old man.''

The words *old man* made the graybeard visibly stiffen. He was growing more irate moment by moment.

"They was in that jail over there. One kept hollering for water and my christian soul demanded I help my brother in distress.''

Bucky looked away, completely disgusted, listening with half an ear, the remainder of his mind busy. According to the old man he'd asked the guard to open the door and when he passed in the water the man with the scar had grabbed him by the arm and jerked him inside.

"One of them had a knife. They was searched but he must've had the blade hid in his boot. He put that to my throat and marched all of us outside where he said that if any of us even thought of shooting at them he'd cut my throat."

"Okay, okay," Ed St. Clair said. "I've heard enough. Time we got a move on, huh, Bucky?"

"I've had too much already," Bucky said.

Bucky and his three rode west of town. "They might have got paid off by the robbers," he said slowly, "and let them ride out free. If so, some or all of that stolen railroad money is in Cannonville."

"Not all," Ed St. Clair said. "If the Cannonville bunch took all, the train robbers would have come back and somehow wiped them out. I'd say that if Cannonville was bought off the train robbers would have ridden off with more than half of their stolen money."

"You got a good point there," Bucky said, "but what if they killed the four bandits for their money and their broncs and got all the four Hashknife men had?"

"I'm more inclined to believe Hashknife

bought them off," Jim Black said. "Killing is murder and a serious offense and it would bring Utah law into the town, which is just what those people don't want, Bucky."

"You got a strong point there, Jim," Bucky said.

"They might not even have jailed Hashknife," Cal Holton said. "They might have surrounded Hashknife, demanded money from the robbers, got it and chased them out of town."

Bucky shrugged. "Something's sure fishy. They said the bandits went west. Let's cut for sign there."

They spread out in a circle and walked, leading their broncs, but found no signs of steel-shod hoofs running west. Bucky straightened his aching back and spat on a sagebrush

"They never went north. We'd have met them this morning going to Cannonville if they had. No sign of them going west, either. They've either returned south or gone east."

"Or straight up," Jim Black joked.

Ed St. Clair smiled. "No wings for that group, ever. Let's circle south of town and see what track we can cut?"

Here were many tracks, both of barefooted and shod horses, for this was the trail running south to Lee's Ferry. Bucky had carefully noted the horse tracks in front of the building wherein the men had presumably been held and he'd noticed that one horse had been shod with one shoe having deep caulks and the other having caulks worn almost slick.

Both shoes had been on the bronc's forefeet, for the prints had been close to the tie-rail. Bucky now looked for such tracks but couldn't find them. "Let's ride east of town," he said.

They forded the Paria river, letting their broncs drink, and rode across a meadow with tall grass and came to the barren foothills where again they dismounted and walked bent over peering at the ground.

They'd searched but a few minutes when Bucky said, "Come here, men," and his posse gathered around him.

The tracks were clear here, for the horse had started to climb the hill and his weight had been mostly on his front hoofs as he started the ascent.

"Left forehoof with deep caulks, right

one with an old shoe worn rather slick. Those the hoofmarks you noticed in Cannonville?" Ed St. Clair asked.

Bucky nodded.

"Only one thing wrong," Ed St. Clair said. "The horse with those shoes might not belong to these bandits. He might be some local lad's cayuse and the local boy has ridden this direction."

"Let's look for more tracks," Bucky said.

They didn't look long. Four horsemen had headed at a lope for the eastern mountains. Bucky scowled. "Where are their four relief horses? They claimed down in Cannonville that the Hashknife men took all four horses with them when they rode out."

"They've dumped them to make more speed," Jim Black said, shading his eyes as he stood on the hill and looked down at the Paria river about a half-mile west. "There's four horses down there along the edge of the brush."

The four rode fast toward the river. Sure enough, the four horses bore the ferryman's brand, for he'd shown them the brand back at Lee's Ferry.

Bucky chewed his bottom lip thoughtfully. "They've got their loot on their saddles in either sacks or saddlebags. They'll be wary because now they'll know we're hunting them. I wonder if there's a pass crossing those mountains to the east, the direction they seem to be heading?"

All four studied the high range of mountains ahead, their crowns capped by eternal snow. Scarp rock rose upward, scraggly with pine, and then the timberline came, nothing but glacial ice and talus cones above that point.

"I don't know," Ed St. Clair said, "but there's only one way to find out, Bucky."

"That's right, Ed."

Rifles across saddles, the four headed into the foothills toward the high mountains, a barrier in the east.

Jim Black said, "I wonder if they did pay those Cannonville people off or did honestly escape?"

Bucky shrugged. "Makes no difference now," he said philosophically.

CHAPTER 11

Days were short at this time of the year in the high plateaus. Therefore dusk found them but a few miles into the mountains. They quit tracking because it got dark so soon.

Also tracking was slow here for fear of riding into an ambush, for this was very good *ambushing country,* as Jim Black stated.

Huge granite boulders dotted mountain sides. Ledges jetted out of peaks offering a secure place for a man lying on his belly and firing down. Arroyos and cutbanks could hide a man while he stood level with the round, rifle to his shoulder.

Bucky had also been afraid of a dry-gulching. That night they didn't build a fire for fear it would be seen. They chewed cold jerky beef and drank cold water from a mountain stream as they held a council of war.

"The surprise element was ours but after they got jailed down in Cannonville they knew for sure somebody's on their trail," Bucky summed up. "They've got to clear out fast, they know, or shoot their way out — and they might pick an ambush."

"That means we can't trail directly behind them," Ed St. Clair said. "We got to swing wide and get ahead of them someway and station ourself between them and that pass over east, because their hoofs are heading that direction, Bucky."

"Any moon tonight?" Jim Black asked.

Bucky shook his head. He knew what Black hinted at. They should mount and swing wide and ride around the bandits, if possible. Their horses were dog-tired, with even tough Sandy sometimes dragging his hoofs.

"You mean swing out and ride around them and ambush them, huh?" Bucky said to Black.

"We might be able to do it by ridin' all night, sheriff, although we don't know this country and dark is hard to ride in."

Bucky agreed that that was possible. He pointed out that the bandits had apparently left Cannonville on the broncs they'd ridden in; therefore, the Hashknife cowboys would be astraddle trail-tired horses, also.

"How far ahead of us would you reckon they'd be?" Cal Holton said, chewing tobacco because he couldn't light a cigaret.

"I'd say about ten miles or maybe a bit more," Bucky said. "Our broncs are danged tired, men. I wonder if they can carry us all night."

"We could walk some and rest them that way," Cal Holton said.

Ed St. Clair laughed softly. "I can see myself with raw heels come daylight, for these Justins I wear just weren't made for walking, friends."

"Well, let's go," Jim Black said.

The night was chilly here at this high altitude and at this time of the year. All were thankful that there was no wind. Pines stood high and dark and guarded this lonesome land in brooding silence, the distant wail of a coyote down along the river breaking the sighing of the tall pines and cedar.

They planned it out as carefully as they could without knowledge of the nature of the terrain to be traversed in the dark. They would stay together, for one thing; no man would ever be left alone. For if he broke a leg or had a bronc fall on him and pin him down he'd have no chance alone in this gigantic wilderness.

They would swing to the south and go around the mountain ahead, following a noisy creek that they'd seen tumbling down from that direction. If the robbers were ten or twelve miles ahead in camp they had a chance to be ahead of the Hashknife men by morning as Hashknife pushed toward the pass between the two overtowering peaks.

But if Hashknife kept pushing on during the night Bucky and his posse would have lost necessary ground by making this wide detour. If Hashknife didn't camp for the night, Hashknife would be double its distance ahead by morning because of the posse swinging in the wide circle.

Bucky fixed their position as best he could from the stars. The creek petered out as the posse climbed and finally became a mere spring and then nothing, with the four manhunters standing on a pine-studded ridge, the night cold and alien about them.

"Even the stars look cold," Jim Black said. "I got one blister on my right heel and six on my left."

"You count them?" Cal Holton joked.

Bucky said, "About seven hours before daybreak at this time of the year. This looks like a clear mesa up ahead that lifts to the pass."

Ed St. Clair looked east. "Hell, you can't see any better than me, and it looks like scraggly sagebrush ahead, that's all."

Bucky grinned. "I can hope, can't I?"

"Let's get movin'," Jim Black said. "I don't want to freeze onto this spot. Might be a long time till some other fool wanders over this way and finds me standing up an icicle."

They led their horses, the horses attempting to grab a bite of bunchgrass here and there, jerking their reins hard in hands as they did so. Now and then they looked back west when on some high ridge hoping to see a campfire below but they saw none, much to Bucky's dismay, for the Hashknife men might have not made a night camp but might have pressed on, realizing that time was the essence.

Bucky thought of his warm bed down in Prescott. He wondered how Pauline was getting along. Then he pushed these warm thoughts deliberately aside and concentrated on the job at hand.

Dawn found them on the summit, a gigantic lift of granite peak on either side. Here was much snow but still blue mountain flowers peeped out of the dirty whiteness.

The wind had died down just before dawn. When the sun rose the world suddenly came to glowing color, the green of the pines clashing with the dull gray of the barren upthrusts.

"There may be other planets that have men living on them," Ed St. Clair said, "but I'll bet there's none as purty as this one."

"The world is wonderful," Jim Black said, "but these things called men sure louse it up."

When full daylight came, they looked for horse tracks. The entire pass was snow and therefore tracks would have been easy to see, but there were none and Bucky's heart leaped.

The thieves had not ridden over this pass, and this pass seemed to be the only one for miles and miles. That meant the Hashknife men had made camp below and spent the night or had swung off to the south or north, fearing that Bucky and his posse might try to cut them off in this mountainous defile.

"No horses have gone over this snow at any time," Cal Holton said.

"I wouldn't say any time," Bucky said. "Hoofmarks could be drifted shut, you know, but there was no wind last night, so they're down below us either coming this way or going some other direction."

"What's next, Bucky?" Jim Black asked.

Bucky looked at his men. Ed St. Clair's beard, he noticed, had a touch of gray but Jim Black's beard was as black as his name. Cal Holton's light whiskers were the color of straw and his blue eyes were bloodshot from lack of sleep and hard riding.

"Let's spread out and comb the high

ridges, each man taking his field glasses and hiding his bronc back here where the horse sure won't be seen from below. I think we'd best have somebody stay with the cayuses, huh?" Bucky said.

"That'd be a good job for Jim," Ed St. Clair said. "One of his water blisters must have busted because he walks like he's tromping on eggs."

Jim Black grinned. "With pleasure will I stay behind, Bucky."

Three hours later they saw the four Texans riding slowly toward the pass, their tired horses dragging hoofs, apparently unaware they'd been circled during the night, evidently thinking their pursuers were far behind.

"We could spread out, the three of us, along the trail and come on them on foot with rifles," Cal Holton said.

Bucky shook his head. "Our horses are quite a ways behind us. If we missed or something went wrong they're mounted and we're on foot and they'd outdistance us and escape again."

Both Cal Holton and Ed St. Clair nodded agreement.

"We go back for our horses. Jim rides

with us. We hide out in a half-circle in the brush right about where the trail comes onto that level area below. Brush is thick enough there to hide us and our mounts."

"And give them the old Apache cavalry charge, huh?" Ed St. Clair said.

"That's right," Bucky said.

— The three returned to Jim Black and the horses and mounted rifle steel whispering against leather as Winchesters were pulled from saddle holsters, each man jacking back his rifle lever slightly to see if a new bullet rode in the barrel.

Thus, the four Hashknife men rode into a trap. One moment the only sounds heard were the plod of their horses' hoofs and the low soughing of pines. The next moment the brush erupted with horsemen and the posse was on them.

For one startled moment, the Hashknife men were frozen in saddles, staring at the four lawmen roaring down on them brandishing rifles, and then the tableau broke into roaring, snarling action.

The Texans didn't have time to pull rifles from saddleboots. They only had time to snake six shooters from holsters.

Horses neighed, reared. Horses fought

gouging spurs, harsh reins. Sandy fairly sat on his haunches he stopped so fast, shod forefeet ripping mountain sod.

Bucky saw Cal Holton's big black smash shoulder to shoulder with a Hashknife horse. Both broncs went down in a kicking squealing tangle of hoofs and men.

Cal dived from leather just as his horse fell. The tough special agent tackled his opponent, bearing him to the ground. Bucky saw Cal land on top, fists hard, pistons driving into the bandit's face.

Bucky then saw before him a leering, scar-marked face. He knew that for the first time he stared at J. J. Smith. Despite the hurried action, he glimpsed Jim Black, low in saddle, pumping rifle-lead at a Texan who was squatted in leather, shortgun lancing flame.

Ed St. Clair's rifle also was speaking, the railroad special agent sitting solidly on his horse, his lips peeled back.

Sandy neighed and reared at that moment, and by rearing undoubtedly saved his master's life, for J. J. Smith's bullet, intended for Bucky's midriff, then plowed into the fork of the lawman's saddle.

It was as though a strong man wielding a sixteen-pound sledge had hit the front of the saddle's tree. The blow almost sent the big buckskin falling backwards.

For one long second, Bucky thought that his tough buckskin might pile up, and he unconsciously kicked his boots out of the stirrups, ready to lunge sidewise if the buckskin fell, but Sandy kept his foot and brought his forehoofs slashing down again — and at that moment Bucky's rifle spoke.

He shot across his saddle's fork. He didn't take aim for his rifle was but half-raised. He shot in desperation and with hope and hope was fulfilled, for his rifle-ball slapped the pistol from J. J. Smith's hand.

The .45 flew into space. Bucky rammed Sandy shoulder-to-shoulder with Smith's smaller and lighter bronc, the big buckskin sending the other horse back on his haunches.

Smith's bronc went down the moment Bucky launched himself from the saddle. He landed on top of Smith, who kicked him off and hurriedly rose to his feet, his hand going like lightning to the hilt of the

Bowie knife sheathed at his belt.

Bucky braced his legs wide, holding his rifle by the barrel. He swung it and the stock smashed Smith across the left ear, sending him reeling. Smith was stunned but not out of the fight.

Quickly, Bucky reversed his rifle. This time the heavy barrel came crashing down onto Smith's head. Smith staggered, walked two steps, then plunged unconscious on his face.

Bucky straightened, breathing heavily. All eight saddle-horses stood now with empty saddles, Smith's horse having scrambled to his hoofs. Cal Holton had a tall bandit by the scruff of his neck, pushing the bloody-faced man toward Bucky, who gulped cool mountain air in huge breaths.

Then he saw Jim Black lying flat on his back, a wiry Texan astraddle him, the Texan pumping hard blows into Black's face.

Both Black and the Texan had lost their weapons in the melee. Bucky ran toward Black, his rifle-butt foremost; he brought the curved butt-plate solidly down on the Texan's neck.

The Texan screamed something and went flying from Black, who leaped to his boots and jerked the stunned Hashknife man to his feet.

Where was Ed St. Clair? Bucky whirled, looking for St. Clair. He just as suddenly relaxed for he saw St. Clair coming toward him, his rifle's barrel in the back of a stumbling, bleeding outlaw.

Bucky breathed a thankful sigh. Apparently nobody had been wounded, although all — posse and outlaws — were more or less beat up.

The surprise attack he and his posse had pulled on the outlaws had been the deciding element in the struggle, for things had happened so swiftly and unexpectedly that there'd been little chance to fire weapons.

The money and expensive jewelry the bandits had lifted from the Santa Fe train was in their saddlebags and in gunny sacks tied behind their saddles. The sum was close to twenty thousand in paper money and about thirty thousand in diamonds and other expensive jewelry.

Cal Holton soon had a big black eye, (his left) Ed St. Clair had his upper and bottom lip rather well bruised. Jim Black had his face hammered so much in a few moments both his eyes were almost closed.

Actually, the bandits had suffered less in the fight than the posse, although each of the four definitely bore the visible signs of the struggle.

J. J. Smith informed Bucky that the old patriarch down in Cannonsville had told the truth when he'd said the bandits had escaped by using him as a hostage.

Five days later hunter and hunted — bewhiskered, dirty, tired — rode eight stumbling-weary horses into Milford, Utah, about a hundred and forty miles northwest of where the battle between posse and train-robbers had been staged.

There the eight took the train to Salt Lake City where they would then go to Denver and thence to Raton, New Mexico Territory, on their way west to Prescott, Arizona. This was the shortest route home for Bucky.

Each bandit was handcuffed to a member of Bucky's posse, J. J. Smith sharing handcuffs with Bucky. Salt Lake City had a celebration for the manhunters, as did Denver and Prescott.

Bucky hugged his wife and then sat in his sheriff's chair, legs extended. He swung the swivel chair around so he looked out the big tall windows of his court house office.

The manhunt had taken him almost a month. While he'd been gone Spring had come to the Prescott mountains. Streams ran clear and trout lurked in cool watery recesses. Black and brown bears roamed the hills searching the first berries of the year.

Two of his prisoners had trimmed the lawn. All was green and warm and comfortable.

Bucky O'Neill stretched out his legs. It was good to be home . . . and all in one piece, too.

Without being aware of it, Sheriff Bucky O'Neill fell asleep.

CHAPTER 12

Bucky O'Neill served but one four-year term as sheriff of Yavapai county, declining to run for a second term though undoubtedly he would have won easily for he was very popular with law-abiding citizens.

He had a number of thorns — or burrs — under his legal saddleblanket, though. One consisted of a man who claimed openly to be the West's fastest gun, a man who boasted of the number of men he'd killed either in fair or unfair gunplay.

This man was named Tom Horn. He became notorious throughout the West. He was born in Missouri, 1860, and soon went west to the plains. He was a well-built man of slight stature, willowy and strong.

He was also intelligent. He learned the

Apache tongue from the great Indian scout, Tom Sieber, who admired Horn very much. Horn worked for the U. S. Army as a frontier scout.

Tom wrote later that Sheriff Bucky O'Neill hired him as a deputy sheriff. He later claimed he did much — if not the most — of Bucky's law work, a statement which apparently held no water.

Tom Horn was an excellent cowboy. He was especially good at roping. At this time Prescott started what is still considered the first United States rodeo or stampede, as a bucking bronc contest is sometimes called in the United States.

Tom easily won roping contests. At Phoenix he roped and tied a critter in forty-nine and one-half seconds, then considered a world record but today something to be laughed at by professional rodeo performers.

But Tom's boasting irked Bucky, who by nature was a quiet, reserved man. Bucky had to let Tom go as deputy sheriff and this did not increase the friendship between Horn, who later died a tragic death, and the sheriff of Yavapai county, Territory of Arizona.

Tom was such a good hand with a rope and a bronc that Buffalo Bill Cody wanted him to ride for *Buffalo Bill's Wild West Show and Congress of Rough Riders,* but Tom turned him down because he wanted to remain in the West and not perform before what he called a *bunch of tinhorns.*

After leaving Prescott, Tom Horn became a Pinkerton detective and was very successful at this, although his bosses complained he was too *trigger happy* — in other words he'd rather gun down his victim than bring him in alive.

Even while at Pinkerton, Tom Horn boasted about helping Bucky to the point where it seemed that Tom Horn was the sheriff and Bucky O'Neill a mere deputy and not the reverse.

Another burr under Sheriff Bucky O'Neill's saddleblanket was a wild Arizona Territory cowboy named George. When sober George was a smiling, easy-going cowboy, nothing more, but when drunk, George imagined himself Wild Bill Hickok and Ben Thompson rolled into one to make the world's roughest, fastest, toughest gunfighter.

George went on a spree about every six months, which was often enough for Prescott's saloon keepers and lawmen. He'd punch cows, save this money, and then go on a big celebration, shooting up saloons and acting the badman in earnest.

Two weeks after returning from the manhunt, Bucky saw George ride into Prescott one fine Spring afternoon, his hat back and his spurs and coins in his pocket all a-jingle.

When George rode into the livery barn Bucky went outside where he met George and relieved him of his hardware. George obligingly flipped the sheriff his pistol.

"Never like to use my gun when I fight," George said. "I use my fists."

"Yes, and bottles and chairs and whatever comes within your reach," Bucky said with a smile. "Why get too drunk? The justice-of-the-peace is tired of fining you after each spree."

"I'll bet he is. I keep the court house running with my fines. See you, sheriff."

Bucky had two deputies patroling nights. When the second relieved the first at midnight sharp he was a block away from George's favorite saloon when he heard the breaking of chairs and curses and the sounds of a struggle.

When the deputy broke into the saloon his fellow officer had a hammerlock on George who fought the deputy to get free to finish a fight he'd had with a burly young miner who watched, fists doubled, nose bleeding.

"George started the fight," the saloon owner said.

George gasped, "I don't like miners!"

The deputies dragged George to jail. The justice-of-the-peace next morning fined a sick George ten dollars and cost and made him pay for damage he'd done to the saloon.

Bucky talked to the miner who said he bore George no ill-will. "He was so stewed he didn't know what he was doing," the miner said.

George paid his fine and bill and soon Bucky saw him ride past the courthouse heading for his job on a distant ranch. George waved at Bucky who waved back. Within a few minutes a wild-eyed cowboy rode in madly and said he'd found George dead a mile out of town.

"He's been shot, Mr. O'Neill! He

looked to me like he'd been shot offen his saddle!"

Bucky spoke to a deputy. "Arrest that miner George fought last night and bring him to my office."

"Shucks, that miner never shot George —"

"Arrest him, anyway."

Bucky rode to where George lay bellydown in the trail. Bucky rolled him over. George had been shot through the heart. Bucky got to his feet, belly sour. Laughing George would laugh — and drink and fight — no more.

Bucky went through George's pockets. George's wallet was missing. Bucky knew exactly to the cent how much money George had had in his wallet when Bucky'd given it back to him this morning, for Bucky had counted the money before giving George a receipt when George went to jail.

Bucky found where the ambusher had crouched in the high brush. The killer had worn high heeled riding boots. That meant little. Almost all men in Prescott wore riding boots.

He looked for the cartridge case of a

fired shell but found none. Evidently the ambusher had not jacked the cartridge from his rifle or had jacked it free and put it in his pocket.

Bucky was sure George had been shot with a soft-nosed rifle shell, for the hole in front of George's heart was smaller than the hole left by the bullet where it came out of George's back.

George had also been shot by a man on the ground for the hole in his front was down lower on his body than the hole in his back. The bullet had traversed George's body at an upward angle.

Bucky tied George's body across the saddle on George's horse and led the horse and grisly burden to the town morgue where he found the town coroner waiting. He then went to his office where his deputy held the miner.

"Found him in a saloon," the deputy said.

The miner looked rather rough from George's fists. Both his eyes were black and his bottom lip was cut and twice normal size. The deputy and Bucky had a brief conference in Bucky's private office.

"George's wallet is missing. He had

over sixty dollars in it. The man who shot him wore riding boots. I don't think it was the miner. Has the miner been very chummy with a third person here in town?"

"I don't know. I'll scout around. What'll I do with the miner?"

"Hold him on suspicion in a cell."

The deputy spent the day talking to various persons but discovered nothing new and Bucky went home for supper. His wife was unhappy with his being sheriff.

Pauline had lost three uncles who'd fought for the Union in the Civil War. She didn't want to lose her husband. Bucky realized she feared for his life because she loved him.

Bucky finished supper and went outside but he didn't go to his courthouse office, he went to the Mexican section of Prescott, where he was very popular with the poverty-stricken Latins.

Because he spoke Spanish fluently the Mexicans sometimes came to him with their troubles. He got them jobs on ranches and helped them as much as possible. George had been killed a few roads north of the Mexican shacks near an irrigation ditch where many times the women went for washwater.

Senora Morales sat on a stool in the corner of her adobe shack, her head in her hands, and as her husband opened the door for Bucky the good *senora* looked up, nodded at Bucky, then put her head again in her hands, her round and big shoulders shaking to sobs.

Bucky had got *Senor* Morales a job swamping in a local saloon. "Ever since I came from work she has sat that way," the worried husband told Bucky.

"What is wrong?" Bucky asked in Spanish.

"I do not know, *amigo*. The children say that this forenoon early she went to the canal for water. She came back and has cried like this ever since."

"I wish I could help in some way," Bucky said.

Suddenly the woman raised her head. "I know the name of the man who killed the good young George, but if I tell I know he will kill me!"

"Not while I'm around, Margarita," Bucky said.

Suddenly the husband said, "Ah, now I

understand. She saw the man who killed George and she's been afraid the man might have seen her and would come back and kill her!"

"Si, papa."

"No man will harm you while I live," *Senor* Morales said.

Bucky said, "You can tell me who killed George, Margarita."

"No, for he might then kill you, too — and you are our best friend."

"I thank you for that, Margarita, but the man will not kill me. Within a few moments he will be in jail or dead."

"Our friend speaks the truth, mama."

The woman then gave Bucky the name of the murderer, a drifter who'd drifted into Prescott a few weeks before, and on whom Bucky had ordered his deputies and undersheriff to keep a watchful eye.

Bucky went down saloon row and didn't see his man. He knew where the man stayed and his room number. He went to a small hotel and knocked on a door. He got no answer.

He put his shoulder against the door. It did not give. It was locked. He drew his pistol. He went back a pace and ran ahead, shoulder foremost. The lock tore open. Gun in hand, Bucky barged into the room.

The drifter jerked himself upright in bed, hand going for the pistol under his pillow. Bucky's gun came down across the thin wrist. The drifter howled in pain. Bucky reached under the pillow and got the man's weapon.

"You ambushed and killed George," he flatly accused.

"You're crazy, sheriff. I don't even know the man. Why would I kill a man I don't know?"

"For his money."

The man stared at Bucky. He rubbed the wrist Bucky had hit with his pistol's barrel. Then the man said, "Yes, I killed him for his money — I was drunk, broke — All day — I've been crazy with fear — I'm glad it's over, sheriff."

The killer was sentenced to life in the hell of the territorial prison in Yuma, one of the hottest sections on earth, where he contracted tuberculosis in his stone cell and died within two years.

Bucky released the miner. "This town's too tough for me," the miner said.

"Goodby, folks." He left for good.

Another killing occurred in January, 1893, just before Bucky left office. It had snowed all night but at ten in the morning the storm ceased and Prescott lay under a lovely white blanket.

At about eleven that morning a cowboy rode madly into Prescott, dismounted in front of the courthouse, and ran into Bucky's office, white-faced from the cold and excitement.

"Sheriff, the Haskin brothers — Mike and Slim — They're dead — both of them — out in the sagebrush!"

"Take it easy, Hank," Bucky said. "Sit down and tell me all you know."

Bucky knew that the bachelor Haskin brothers had a small gold mine southwest of Prescott about ten miles.

The cowboy punched cattle for Circle Y southwest of Prescott in the Loma Prieta Mountains. He'd been hunting strays and had run across the bodies of the Haskin brothers about a mile from the Oro Fino store where the cowboy'd been riding because he'd run out of Bull Durham.

"They must have been goin' to the Oro Fino store when somebody shot them both in the back."

Bucky reached for his rifle. "Why shot in the back, cowboy?"

"Soft-nosed bullets, sheriff. Bigger hole in the front of their heads than behind. I'll ride with you and show you where the bodies were moved to, sheriff."

"Where are they now?"

"I notified the Oro Fino store. Storekeeper said it weren't right for dead men to lay aroun' an' he'd move the corpses to his store."

Bucky buckled on his spurs. He silently wished the bodies had not been moved for he'd wanted to study them as they'd fallen, but it was too late now. Some do-gooder always seemed to louse up a sheriff's job.

He picked up his rifle. "Let's go, cowboy."

The two murdered brothers lay on the floor in the store's back room. Both had been shot from behind the head with soft-nosed bullets, as the cowboy had stated.

The cowboy then took Bucky to the spot where the bodies had lain. Bucky could find no tracks because the harsh wind had whipped sand around and there was no snow.

Evidently the brothers had been on foot; no horses were around. Bucky found no fired cartridge cases, either. He and the cowboy returned to the store, a sudden thought hitting him.

"Didn't the Haskins have a nephew come in from back East to visit them about a week ago?" Bucky asked of the storekeeper.

It paid to keep track of humans. He had a deputy who met each stage and watched passengers board each stage out.

"Yes, he's visiting the brothers. Yes, I saw him just this mornin'. He was waitin' outside this mornin' when I opened up at my usual time, seven. He bought a box of .30-30 ca'tridges off'n me. He had his rifle with him."

"Hard-nosed or soft-nosed bullets?" Bucky asked.

"Soft-nosed, sheriff. Wonder how long them two been dead?"

"I don't know, but they're stiff with *rigor mortis.* Will you draw me a rough map showing me how to get to their mine?"

"Be glad to, sheriff."

The cowboy bought his Bull Durham and went about his business. "Sometimes that nephew acts kinda loony. He's jus' a kid, you know."

Bucky easily found the mine but he didn't ride directly up to the opening in the mountain. He hid Sandy in the brush and went ahead on foot, Winchester in hand.

It hardly seemed possible that the nephew had been so stupid that he'd murdered his two uncles, and Bucky wondered, if this had come about, what had motivated the nephew to commit murder.

The only thing he could think of was that the nephew, if he'd murdered his uncles, had done so for the gold taken from this mine. Bucky knew that wasn't much for not much gold ore was in this hardrock vein.

Hidden in mesquite he studied the mine's opening forty feet ahead — a black hole blasted into gray granite. Two steel rails led into the mine. That told him the brothers Haskins had a mine-ore car which they used to haul ore from the bowels of the earth.

The car was not in sight. That told Bucky the car was in the mine. Suddenly he cocked his head and listened intently, what he heard did not seem logical — for somebody inside was hitting quartz with a pick!

Was the nephew inside working the mine? That hardly seemed logical. Had the nephew murdered his uncles surely he'd have fled by now? Bucky then remembered the level-headed Oro Fino storekeeper as mentioning that he considered the nephew a loony.

Bucky decided to wait it out. He had to wait thirty or so minutes. His feet were cold. His knuckles were blue as they clutched his rifle. Finally the nose of the ore-car appeared.

The car was pushed by a short youth with the beginnings of red whiskers. Bucky quickly noticed a rifle lying across the chunks of ore.

He waited until the youth had his back toward him and then he stepped out, rifle up and ready, for he had learned early in his sheriff duties you took no chances. If you did, you'd not finish the end of your term.

"Okay, nephew. Forget that rifle or I'll kill you! Put your hands high! Now turn around ~~the turn~~ slow and keep your hands up, savvy!"

The man jumped, turned, stared. "Remember," Bucky said, "hands high, nephew!"

The hands shot upward. "Who are you?"

Bucky introduced himself. "You killed your two uncles this morning, didn't you?"

"Yes, I killed them."

Bucky realized the storekeeper was right. This young man was not normal mentally. "Why did you murder them?"

"I wanted this mine. Now I own it."

Bucky said, "Stay as you are. Don't move." He reached out for the rifle on the ore-car. He never got it.

He'd never seen a man as fast as this insane youth. One second, one lightning move — and the loony had the rifle. He was raising it when Bucky, who'd fallen to one knee, shot the rifle from the youth's hand, the Winchester flying away with a bullet-shattered stock.

When the prisoner reached Prescott, Bucky put him in a cell and called the doctor. He got the address and name of the youth's father and then wired the father in New York City, the father wiring back that his son had escaped from a mental hospital and all this time he'd wondered where his son had been.

Judge Pinney's successor committed the youth to the state mental hospital but many nights thereafter Bucky awakened bathed with cold sweat, realizing how close the youth had come to shooting his rifle.

Two weeks later, Bucky O'Neill again tangled with some tough Texans. This time he didn't have the steady gunhand and rocklike Marshal Garfias to aid him. He tamed the Texans by himself.

These Texans worked for a Tonto Basin outfit. Two weeks before Bucky and his undersheriff had jailed four of the Texans for being drunk and disorderly. The Texans hadn't had money to pay their fines. Bucky accordingly put them to work on the county work gang for a week.

The Texans were forced to do manual labor under guard on Prescott's streets.

Little boys jeered them. The Texans were hurt where it hurt the most . . . in their Lone Star pride.

The leader — a tall, strawheaded man of twenty-five — had ridden out of Prescott swearing he'd return and put the hide of one Yavapai County sheriff on the home-outfit's bunkhouse wall.

Bucky knew the Texan meant every word . . . and he was prepared, but the Texans evidently had an informant staked out in Prescott, for they rode in to take Sheriff Bucky O'Neill apart when Bucky's undersheriff and deputy were both out of town on official business, the first time Bucky'd been left alone to uphold the law for months and months.

Six Texans bucked broncs into Prescott at dusk. Six-shooters blasted holes in the air and around the dust of scurrying frightened townspeople. Rebel yells split the mountain air.

As usual, Bucky sat in his office in front of the big window. From this vantage point he could command a view of almost the entire town. He immediately recognized the riders as Texans because a flaxen-haired rawboned blue-eyed young

221

man rode lead saddle, big stetson back as he whooped and blasted his gun upward.

The Texans dismounted in front of Cavanaugh's Saloon, one of Prescott's biggest and wildest. They didn't tie their horses to the hitchrack but told a townsman to tie them or they'd weight him down with lead.

To emphasize the order the blond youth fired his last bullet at the townsman's boots, making splinters fly from the plank sidewalk. The townsman leaped for the reins. The Texans laughed and entered Cavanaugh's, the blond youth reloading his six-shooter.

Bucky got slowly to his feet. His face was calm but his heart beat heavily. He checked his six-shooter and retied it lower on his hip. Then he picked up his Stetson and left to cross the street to Cavanaugh's, wishing he had a deputy or two to side him.

Townsmen had fled out Cavanaugh's rear door. Bucky paused for a moment in front of the saloon to listen. He heard the light-haired man say, "Bring on that goddamned fire-eating sonofabitchin' marshal or sheriff or whatever the bastard is!"

Bucky realized odds were six to one against him. He realized he should have entered the saloon with his gun in his hand but if he did so the Texans would claim he'd taken unfair advantage of them.

He also knew that these sons of the Lone Star had a strong sense of fair play. He felt that if he challenged the flaxen-haired man the others would stand back and let him and the blond fight it out together without interference.

Therefore his gun was in holster when he barged into the saloon, hastily entering and moving quickly to his left, for he feared a man or two might be in a position to rap him over the skull from behind as he entered.

But all six Texans were lined up at the bar, the blond closest to Bucky and the door. Cavanaugh's bartender was in the act of pouring the blond a drink.

When the bartender saw Bucky his arm froze in a crooked fashion as though death had struck the man and congealed him into this awkward position. For one long moment there was silence as the

Texans turned their heads and looked at the lone lawman.

Slowly, carefully, the bartender lowered his hand — and the bottle. He then retreated, walking backwards, and when close to the rear door he turned and bolted, breaking the stiff silence that had momentarily held the Texans and Bucky.

Bucky's blue eyes collided with the Texan's blue eyes. Bucky realized that of the six this blond was the only one who'd worked on the street gang; therefore, the others didn't bear toward him the intense hate the blond bore him.

The blond also apparently was the Texan's leader. Bucky figured that if he tamed the flaxen-haired rider he'd not have much trouble with the other five, for plainly none of the six had been drinking.

Bucky said to the blond, "You're under arrest, Texan. The charge is bucking your bronc down the street, cursing and firing your pistol promiscuously."

"You won't get me back on your street gang," the big man said. "You won't put me in a position where a damned Yankee can spit on a Texan again!"

"The Civil War was over more than

twenty-five years ago," Bucky said, "and according to the papers we're getting ready for another with Spain, but that's neither here nor there."

"What's your point?" the light-haired rider demanded.

"You said you'd nail my hide to your bunkhouse wall. I face six to one odds but you boys are Texans, and Texans have always had the reputation of being honest and square-shooting men.

"That's right, tin star," the big Texan said.

Bucky had gained a point. He pressed his case further with, "That being true, you'll face me and face me alone, Texan."

The Texan's pride had walked him into a trap. He couldn't back out and save his stiff-necked pride.

"You an' me alone, tin badge," he growled.

Bucky chose words with care, aware that the other five Texans were moving away from the light-haired man. "My gun's in my holster. Yours is in your leather. You loaded it as you came in because I saw you. That puts it man to man, doesn't it, Texan?"

"That's right," the Texan said.

Now all the other riders were far to the side, leaving Bucky and the flaxen-haired rider alone. The light-haired Texan moved away from the bar, always facing Bucky, who stood with his hand on his gun, crouched suddenly and with his eyes never leaving his adversary.

Then, the Texan stopped moving, his position found. He put his right boot slightly ahead of his left, the way a prizefighter handles his feet. Then he sank down slowly into a gunman's crouch, his body low and slanted to provide the least possible target.

Then the Texan said, "I'm comin' at you, O'Neill!"

The two men drew almost simultaneously, witnesses peering through windows later related, but the Texan shot too fast, something Bat Masterson had cautioned Bucky O'Neill against.

Also, the Texan didn't know the trick of pointing your forefinger along your pistol's barrel, the barrel automatically following the path of your pointing. He missed and Bucky shot.

There were just two shots fired.

Bucky's bullet broke the man's gunarm. He dropped his gun, the Texan did; he grabbed his right forearm, blood spurting from between his fingers.

"My God, O'Neill. If you've cut one of my arteries —" Fear of death rode the young man's twisted face.

Bucky swung his gun to cover the other five, but they stood with raised hands, evidently wanting none of this sheriff-gunman. Somebody had left early for the town doctor, who forced the wounded man into a chair and opened his bag and began sponging.

Finally the doctor looked up. "Both bones broken, Bucky, but no artery cut. Damn it, when will men learn to live in peace?"

"If that happened you'd lose a lot of trade, sawbones," a young Texan said, "and the men making money off bullets and wars wouldn't be happy. What about us, O'Neill?"

Bucky actually now hated to arrest any of the men, but the law required he do so, for they'd broken the town ordinance of bucking broncs on the streets and firing pistols promiscuously.

The doctor took the wounded man to his office. Bucky took the other five across the street to the courthouse and the justice-of-the-peace hurriedly called court into session, fining each man three dollars each.

"No more than three bucks?" a surprised Texan asked, digging up three silver dollars.

"That's all," Bucky said. "Leave your guns here. This office is open all night. Resume your drinking but watch your manners, boys."

They all grinned and shook hands. Later Bucky dropped into the saloon district. The cowboys were drinking and having a good time, even the one with the broken arm.

The flaxen-haired man shook Bucky's hand with his left hand, his right being encased in plaster-of-paris. "Boss won't get much work out of me for a while," he said, grinning. "I can't even make a good kitchen flunky. Who the hell can peel a spud with one hand?"

He and Bucky both laughed. Later many Texans came into Prescott but each acted, thereafter, in a *rather gentlemanly manner,* as the town schoolteacher described it.

The Texas trouble was over in Prescott.

CHAPTER 13

The fall of 1893 Bucky O'Neill ran for the office of Territorial Representative after declining to again run for the office of sheriff. He was severely beaten at the polls for he'd been unhappy and dissatisfied with both the Republican and Democratic tickets and had run on the Popular Ticket. Even without a political post though, his days were busy.

The Territory had licensed him to practice law so he hung out his shingle and edited *Hoofs and Horns,* which rather rapidly grew into an Arizona standby because it entered the home of every man who had a brand in the Territory, and almost each man had one or two head of cows or horses.

Prescott still had no railroad so *Hoofs and Horns* plunged into an editorial campaign to get a railroad down from Ashfork on the north. Bucky, while sheriff, discovered that the arrogant Santa Fe railroad had not for years paid taxes on the land the Territory had given the company for building across Arizona.

Bucky, as a taxpayer, filed a suit against the railroad, asking that present taxes and back taxes be paid. He'd learned as sheriff that many times a politician had to compromise and his plan was to force Santa Fe to build down to Prescott from Ashfork if the county cancelled the back taxes due from Santa Fe.

Arrogant railroad officials paid him no attention until he brought them into the county court, where *Hoofs and Horns* lost its case. Railroad officials conferred with him. If they built down from Ashfork, he'd drop the suit. They made no promises.

When *Hoofs and Horns* appealed the county court's decision to the district court Santa Fe realized Bucky O'Neill meant business, for *Hoofs and Horns* opponent, the *Courier,* also took up the fight.

High-priced lawyers cost Santa Fe much

money while Bucky handled his own suit. Finally the railroad compromised. Rails down from Ashfork reached Prescott in 1893.

Hoofs and Horns then put pressure on Southern Pacific to build up to Prescott from the south, thus giving Prescott access to two mainline railroads. Because Southern Pacific had no property in Yavapai County no tax suit could be filed against it.

The *Courier* joined forces with *Hoofs and Horns* again. Bucky was called by Southern Pacific to Phoenix to discuss matters. He and Price Behan made the trip by stage. Behan was the head of the Yavapai County Commissioners.

Behan was a close friend — a thickset good-looking man four years Bucky's senior. Heavy clouds scurried across the Arizona sky that spring day when Behan and Bucky boarded the horse-drawn stage for Phoenix. Two other men and their wives were passengers with Bucky and Behan.

The time of departure was ten minutes gone when Bucky asked, "Where's the driver?"

"He's in Cavanaugh's Saloon," a woman said.

Bucky spoke to Price Behan. "Maybe I should go in and drag him out?" The idea of a half-drunk or drunken stagedriver didn't appeal to him, for there were some stiff hills and wicked cut-coulees in the mountains south of Prescott.

"He'll be along soon," good natured Price said. "We're not in that much of a hurry, Bucky."

Five minutes later the saloon's batwing doors opened. The driver came out and ran for his stage and Bucky thought his footing was a little uncertain, but he made no comment.

The stage started with a jerk, the driver's lash crackling over the broad backs of his four horses hooked two abreast. The lunging forward force drove some passengers forward and others back hard against the leather-covered seats.

Bucky straightened, frowning.

The stage left Prescott on the dead run, the horses with ears back as steel-shod hoofs scattered gravel and dust. It rocked violently around a corner and then leveled out for the straight run down off the mountain.

Passengers hung on for dear life. The women were pale and the men not much more tan.

"Hooray for Jeff Davis!" the driver whooped, whip snapping viciously.

A woman snapped, "The idiot doesn't know the Civil War is over. I wish I was home in my living room."

"Don't worry, Sadie," her husband said.

"I wonder if we'll get to Phoenix alive?" the second housewife said, voice trembling.

"I hope so," her husband said.

Bucky harbored some doubts about reaching Phoenix without a stage crackup, for the driver had his teams on the dead run, the stage lurching dangerously on its leather thoroughbraces.

He glanced at Price. Price's lips were set and his eyes growing dangerously narrow and when good natured Price got his dander up it was time to run for the hills.

Price looked out at the passing countryside. "Been raining in the mountains ahead, it looks like. If it has, Agua Fria River might have quite a bit of floodwater in it.''

Bucky knew that when flash-rainstorms hit the mountains the water ripped over boulders and hit Agua Fria River in no time, sometimes suddenly raising the roaring mountain river to flood heights.

Bucky said, "Don't cross a river until you come to it."

Price dug out a cigar. The stage lurched so much he had difficulty lighting it, a fact that brought a low angry grunt from the politician-cattleman.

Finally Price got his cigar lit and leaned back and blew smoke out the open window so it wouldn't bother the two women passengers. Soon the stage rocked into the mountains, wheels grinding on loose gravel.

One woman shielded her eyes with her handkerchief so she'd not look into the deep abyss a few inches to the right of the lunging wheels.

Finally the Concord successfully left the mountains. It roared down on Dutchman Flats, a level area about three miles long.

Usually the stage hit it fast across the Flats for usually it lost time in the mountains — but not today, for the driver pulled his sweaty horses to a long trot and settled back on his high seat taking life easy, a bottle close to his hand.

A hundred yards from the upward grade on the south end of Dutchman Flats the driver hollered down, "Hang on, folks. I gotta make up for lost time. Here we go!"

The stage lurched, passengers hanging onto each other and everything they could find, both women screaming up at the driver.

Price Behan glanced inquiringly at Bucky O'Neill.

Bucky shook his head. "We can't climb up and jump him on this rough grade, Price. There might be a fight up there and all might go over the grade, stage and humans and horses!"

Price put his mouth close to Bucky's ear. "When we come to the flat country we climb up and jump him!"

Bucky nodded.

Finally, after what seemed eternity, the stage left the mountains and thundered across a flat-topped mesa. Bucky slid out one window, grabbing the baggage rail on top, and Price went out the other.

They came onto the Concord behind the

unsuspecting driver who had the reins tied loosely around the brake-handle and who was, at that moment, taking a long suck from his quart bottle which Bucky noticed was half empty.

The bottle had been full when the driver had run for the stage back in Prescott.

"You get the bottle, Price," Bucky hollered. "I'll get the reins!"

For the first time, the driver was aware of men behind him. He stood up and Price Behan wrenched the bottle from his surprised hand. Bucky gave the driver a hard shoulder-block.

The man screamed and went backwards, tumbling from the stage. As Bucky grabbed the ribbons he looked back to see the man rolling in the dust. He pulled the team to a slow halt, made a wide circle in the gray sagebrush, and drove back to where the driver sat in the sand, a stupid and drunken look on his homely face.

"Thank God for you two men," a woman said.

Behan looked at Bucky. "What'll we do with the sot? We can't leave him out here for coyotes to nibble on?"

"Gag him and tie him hand and foot and throw him in the boot," Bucky said.

"You cain't do that," the driver said hurriedly. "They's suitcases in the boot."

"Don't worry about that," Bucky assured. "Price and I will ride on the box and pilot the stage into Phoenix so we can load the suitcases inside on the seats we two were sitting on!"

"I promise to drive good from here on in," the drunk said. He tried to get to his boots, fell sidewise, tried to rise again and again failed. "I must've busted a leg."

When the stage started again Bucky tooled the ribbons, Price riding beside him on the high box, the drunken driver gagged and bound hand and foot in the boot behind the stage.

Half an hour later the Concord came to the west bank of the Agua Fria River. True to Price Behan's prediction, the river ran wild at muddy flood stage. Bucky pulled his horses to a halt with the lead team out in the shallow water while all four panting horses drank.

Rock Spring Station was just across the river in the dense grove of big cottonwoods. The station operator hollered something over but nobody heard it because of the roar of the high waters.

A man stuck his head out of the stage and called up, "Think it's too deep, men?"

Bucky looked at Price, who knew this crossing better than he, for Price ran cattle in this section and had crossed at this ford many times, both on horseback and with rigs.

"Not too high," Price Behan said, studying the water. "You know the crossing, Bucky?"

"Pretty well. There's a gravel bar running out from the other side. A horse has to swim about forty feet and then his forehoofs hit it and he pulls himself onto it and is as good as across."

"That's it. I'll get some rocks to throw at the cayuses."

Bucky knew the bottom was solid, all gravel. The danger would come when the teams had to swim for the hard current might sweep the stage downstream or overturn it.

Bucky realized water might flow through the stage. Both he and Price didn't happen to think of the drunk in the boot which was even lower down than the stage's floor.

"Here we go," Bucky said, standing up with boots braced wide. "Throw the rocks, Price. Hip, hip, cayuses."

Price threw rocks at the horses for Bucky couldn't handle the whip and the reins at the same time in such a precarious situation and Price, if he handled the lash, might accidentally hit Bucky with it were Bucky to make an unexpected move.

The lead team took the torrent gingerly but soon were in bellydeep. Bucky heard somebody praying down in the stage. He was surprised to discover it was a man's voice and not a woman's.

Crossing this flooded stream required careful driving, not speed. Water smashed against the wheels. Bucky prayed that no stray log or dead cow would suddenly be washed hard against the stage to upturn it.

Steel ground on gravel. The horses pulled faithfully, ears back. Then they hit the spot where they had to swim. This was where the danger lay. The horses had no footing. The stage for a moment would be a boat, floating with wheels not touching bottom.

"Here we go," Price Behan said.

Bucky pounded his broncs with reins, begging them for more speed at this point. The lead team took to the water and swam like hunting dogs and the second team soon was also swimming.

The coach came to the deep spot. Water washed over the floor boards. The current swung it slightly, its back end pointing slightly downriver. For a moment it looked touch and go. Bucky's heart was in his throat. A few more seconds and the stage would roll over because of the stiff side current —

Then, the lead team's front hoofs caught on the gravel bar and the horses lunged ahead to gain secure footing for their hind hoofs also.

Then the lead team, hoofs thoroughly braced on hard gravel, fairly pulled the second team and the Concord to safety, much to Bucky's relief. Within a few minutes the horses dripping water and the stage rolled to a halt before the log relay station.

Here fresh horses would be hooked to the Concord. Bucky got down and opened the door for the grateful passengers who'd stood on seats and didn't even have wet feet.

Suddenly Bucky looked at Price Behan, mouth sagging open. "Good lord, Price! The driver — in the boot —!"

Both came instantly alive. The driver could have been drowned. They tore open the boot's double doors. The driver lay inside sopping wet, trying to say something around his gag.

Bucky and Behan pulled the man out and jerked off his bandana gag. The man spouted water, muttering curses, but he seemed to have sobered up, the cold water possibly bringing him to his senses.

"You almost drown'ded me!" he accused, looking about. "I'm purty sober now. I think I can take the rig into Phoenix."

Hoofs and Horns was successful in its struggle to get a railroad running southeast from Prescott to Phoenix. Within a few years the line was laid and Prescott had rail connections with two transcontinental railways.

Then came war.

CHAPTER 14

Bucky O'Neill was elected mayor of Prescott in fall of 1897 at the age of thirty-seven. The job was more honorary than active and he'd recently sold *Hoofs and Horns* so he had some time to write.

He was working on a short story in his study when a neighbor brought in news that the *Maine* had been sunk in Havana. For some years war clouds had been on the horizon, the United States government proclaiming the Spanish treated Cubans and other Latins — including the Philippines — like slaves.

"You sure this is true?" Bucky asked. "It's not another rumor, is it?"

The neighbor reported the news had just come up the wire from Phoenix and was posted on the depot bulletin board. Bucky thought of his wife and her hatred toward strife and war.

"Uncle Sam isn't takin' this layin' down," the neighbor said.

"Maybe it'll blow over," Bucky said.

But the trouble grew worse. A corps of American naval officers investigated the *Maine* incident and concluded that the battle ship had been torpedoed. President McKinley stated on April 19, 1898, that in the eyes of the United States Cuba was a free and independent nation.

Spain then declared war on the United States for Spain could do nothing else. The next day the United States Congress returned the favor and declared war on Spain.

Prescott cheered this news with skyrockets and whooping and hollering, especially after Theodore Roosevelt resigned as Assistant Secretary of Navy to organize a fighting cavalry unit called Rough Riders.

Bucky immediately thought of his mounted police unit, the Prescott Grays. He wired Roosevelt immediately offering the services of his cavalry group. Roosevelt never answered the telegram.

Roosevelt was very popular with the

common people. He was a hunter, sportsman, a former rancher and seemingly an all-around fellow. He stated that the Rough Riders would consist of cowboys, Indians and polo players from the east, which Bucky allowed was quite a combination.

Commodore George Dewey on May 1 began firing at dawn into the Spanish fleet which he'd bottled up in Manila Harbor and within a few hours had sunk the entire Spanish *armada*.

Bucky was afraid the war would be over before he got into it, for he realized that if he ever became much in Arizona politics he'd have to have a war record, even if this record consisted solely of sitting behind a desk in Washington safely pushing a pen.

Democrat Myron McCord was then Arizona's territorial governor and he had little use for Bucky because Bucky had bolted the Democratic party to run on the Popular ticket for territorial representative.

Despite these political differences, though, Bucky fully expected to be appointed to one of the captain posts

Roosevelt had allotted to Arizona, for these two captains in the Rough Riders would organize that corps for Arizona.

Governor McCord immediately appointed a political crony, Jim McClintock, as one captain, but hesitated about appointing the other, a fact which brought an irate Bucky O'Neill to Phoenix. The territorial capital had been moved from Prescott to Phoenix in 1889, a move Bucky and Prescott citizens had fought diligently against.

McCord then promised to appoint Bucky the second captain. Bucky returned happily to Prescott. Days and days went by but no official acknowledgement of his being appointed came to Bucky in Prescott, but Bucky found consolation in the fact that the appointment of Jim McClintock had not been made official in Washington, either.

Meanwhile many Arizonians expected the Prescott Grays to be the corps of the Rough Riders. Cowboys rode in from all directions. Within a few days the Grays consisted of over eight hundred riders. Prescott was full of cowboys. Never before — even at rodeo time — had the town had so many cowboys in it.

Washington wired Phoenix that Arizona's allotment in the Rough Riders would be a mere one hundred and twenty cowboys. Bucky immediately wired Roosevelt that he personally commanded eight hundred tough, hard-riding, hard-fighting cowboys. Again Roosevelt disdained to answer.

Roosevelt's disdain and failure to reply irked Bucky, of course, and other news came in to rub him raw, also. Some of this news concerned Bucky's past big-mouthed deputy, Tom Horn, who had gained quite a reputation as a manhunter and gunfighter . . . at least the way Tom Horn told it.

He'd occasionally seen Horn at various lawman and other conventions, for Horn was a great publicity seeker. Whether he and Horn ever had hard words over Horn's mouth is not known, but it is known that Bucky had little, if any, respect for Horn, for Bucky did not like men who boasted of shooting men from ambush, even if the man were drunk while making the boast . . . something Tom Horn had not been.

Tom Horn was now in Wyoming, still working for Pinkerton Detective Agency. He'd aligned himself with the big powerful Wyoming Cattleman's Association to fight off the small farmer and small cowmen, for Horn went on the side that paid the most money — in other words, he sold his gun to the highest bidder, another point that appealed not a bit to Bucky O'Neill.

Bucky heard that Tom Horn had applied to the Army as a scout but of course there was no need for scouts in Cuba. Tom had been a scout for the Army during the Apache trouble and apparently he wished to carry on this same profession during this war.

Bucky knew that Tom Horn disliked discipline and the Army, of course, had strict discipline. Therefore word came to Bucky that Horn had applied for the job of packer for the Army and the Army had accepted him immediately for had he not been a professional packer as a youth for the cavalry when it fought Geronimo and other Apache chiefs?

The Army was organizing its pack unit in St. Louis, Missouri, and Missouri was

Horn's home state, Bucky remembered. Bucky learned that Tom Horn was soon made head packer — and the Army had but sixteen men in this rank. Word came to Bucky that Roosevelt was reading Thackeray's *Vanity Fair*. This irked Bucky more than ever. Why the heck didn't Roosevelt answer the wire Bucky had dispatched him?

Bucky's confirmation as captain didn't come through, neither did that of McClintock. Then to the surprise of Bucky, McClintock and all of Prescott, an army lieutenant arrived in Prescott and opened an enlistment office on April 28.

Bucky realized then that both he and McClintock had been shoved aside and he was the first in line to enlist when the enlistment office opened in the morning. He was, in fact, the first man to enlist in the United States for the Spanish-American War.

He enlisted as a private but his commission came through within a few days and he was promoted to captain at a banquet in Phoenix. His unit was called to leave on May 4.

Prescott gave him and his boys a wild

farewell. Bucky and his Rough Riders pranced horses down the main street, thousands standing to cheer. Saloons were full and churches empty.

Bucky, as mayor, made a speech wherein he temporarily resigned his official position, and then the horses and cowboys were in a boxcar rolling fast toward Phoenix and the mainline of the Southern Pacific which would take them to the point of debarkation in Florida.

Bucky's effort in entering the service had been slow and uncertain, but from now on to Cuba everything seemingly went wrong. The Rough Riders would train briefly at San Antonio, Texas, where some extra broncs would be broken for the Cuban invasion.

Here Roosevelt ordered commanders to give Rough Riders foot-drills, a point each cowboy loathed. Roosevelt's reputation and appeal was falling a few degrees each week in Bucky's estimation.

Prescott citizens had given each Rough Rider a new Colt .45 pistol. Here in San Antonio each was given a new Krag-Jorgenson carbine, a short-barreled rifle that could easily be carried on a saddle.

Rough Riders were also issued uniforms of brown khaki trousers and blue heavy flannel shirts, much too heavy for San Antonio's high humidity heat. Each Rough Rider was also assigned a gray slouch hat. Some hats were too tight, some fit, some fell over ears. There ensued much trading of hats.

Bucky once again encountered Tom Horn for Horn was also encamped in San Antonio where he was a pack master. The two men had not seen each other for some time and they shook hands warmly, whatever ill-natured feelings existing between them evaporating under the stress of their nation at war.

Both men had matured since the days of Tom Horn being Bucky's deputy. Each was now in his late thirties but their ways of living had drifted further and further apart with each passing month.

Bucky had become a useful citizen — a newspaper man, a lawman, a family man, a useful member of Arizona Territory's political family — while Tom Horn had drifted further and deeper into the habit of killing and killing again. Although he appeared calm and unruffled on the surface, underneath his litheness lurked the desire to kill — a thirst which in turn would lead him to the gallows directly after the Spanish-American War was ended.

Uncle Sam was sending eight pack trains to Cuba. One hundred and nine packers would take care of the mules. Of these one hundred and nine, sixteen were pack masters and eight were chief packers.

Bucky learned that Tom was a pack master and soon would be promoted to chief packer, for Tom knew mules. Tom's years with the army mule-packing from various frontier posts had given the detective much experience with mules.

Each pack train consisted of a chief packer, two pack masters, twenty packers and a hundred long-eared stubborn mules. Along with the mules was a mare that carried an always-ringing bell.

Oddly, mules were attracted to mares, even though mules were hybrids and unable to reproduce. Once closely associated with a mare a mule will gladly follow her wherever she cares to go and will follow as closely as possible, as though led by a tie-rope.

Tom carried a pair of sole-leather goggles over his right shoulder. These were used to blindfold mules that were ornery and wanted to kick, bite and strike out with forehoofs.

When a mule had the goggles fitted over his eyes of course he couldn't see and a mule that cannot see doesn't know just which way to kick to contact another mule or human flesh.

Bucky had blindfolded broncs many times with his vest, one reason cowboys in those days invariably wore vests, for a vest made a perfect blindfold while a mean horse was being saddled and mounted.

You fitted the bronc's ears through the armholes in the vest. His ears thus fitted, the vest of course covered his eyes. You could then button the vest under his jaw or leave it hanging loose from his ears for at his best he could only glimpse a bit of daylight either overhead or by looking down the vest at the ground below.

Tom told Bucky that he had no love for Army life. He'd hoped to get into the fray as a civilian but inasmuch as no scouts were needed or hired he'd had to enlist and thus become a mule packer.

He told Bucky that when the war was over he'd return to Wyoming and Montana and Colorado and that locality to again work for the Cattleman's Association or the Pinkertons.

Tom grinningly related that he'd again met an old Arizona frontier fort commander he'd known, one General William R. Shafter. He'd met General Shafter sitting on the veranda of a San Antonio hotel surrounded by dark-skinned Latin beauties.

Tom related that General Shafter had grown very fat and soft and he wondered what use, if any, the General would be in the steaming hot Cuban jungle. Tom Horn and Bucky O'Neill carried not an extra ounce of fat and were flat-bellied and hard-muscled from outdoor life and lots of hard work and hours spent in the saddle — for whoever saw a fat cowboy?

Tom Horn wished the war was over. He was lonesome for the wide limitless spaces of Montana, Wyoming and Colorado, where a man could ride for miles and miles and never see barbwire or be forced to pass through a gate. And in this respect he and Bucky O'Neill saw eye to eye.

For Bucky was lonesome for the mountains and high pines and swift rivers and creeks of his adopted Arizona Territory. This San Antonio, Texas country was more Southern than Western in his eyes. The people spoke with a southern drawl and half the town was Latin, transplanted Mexicans.

You heard more bastard Spanish on the streets then you did English. Sometimes a man thought he was in Mexico and not the United States, Bucky reasoned. And the climate —

The weather was damp and hot and very uncomfortable. It was as hot — if not hotter! — at midnight than it was at noon. Then toward morning it would get so billy-hell chilly your teeth would rattle.

Arizona had four climates a year. This section of the Lone Star State had *four climates in one day!* You sweated one hour and shivered from cold the next. Many of the Arizona cowboys had colds and some suffered from respiratory ailments due to the high humidity, for they were desert men used to breathing dry and clean and healthy desert air.

Bucky hadn't lived in such humid

conditions since leaving home in Virginia. When night came you fairly peeled one blanket from the other for they were that stiffly stuck together with dampness.

Word came that Teddy Roosevelt had finished *Vanity Fair,* at long last. Bucky knew that the Thackeray novel was very long, for he'd tried to read it, but it had been so dull he'd soon thrown it aside. "What's he reading now?" he asked Tom Horn.

Tom grinned as he made a half-hitch around the bony nose of a stubborn mule. "I don't know, O'Neill, but I sure hope it's a manual of war, not another novel!"

All expected to see Teddy Roosevelt in camp. Roosevelt was never seen. For three weeks Arizona men drilled on foot and broke broncs, the latter being more favored than the former.

Word came to break camp on a Sunday, May 29, and rumor said they were being shipped to Florida to board a boat with their horses for Cuba. War had moved closer. To Bucky it didn't seem so glamorous now, as he wrote home to his patient wife and his growing son.

Again, broncs were led up ramps into

boxcars. Finally San Antonio was behind. Regulations demanded horses be watered and fed and stretched every twelve hours but the railroad company paid this order no heed.

"Teddy can't run the Southern Pacific," a cowboy said. "The railroad's bigger even than Teddy."

Finally the first rest stop occurred. The train jarred to a halt in Louisiana. The railroad had no facilities for watering and feeding the horses or men. They'd even forgotten the leading ramps back at San Antonio.

Bucky groaned in anger and weariness. This wasn't turning out like it had promised. A few men openly cursed Teddy. Had a man dared curse Teddy when that man had been leaving Prescott another Rough Rider would have belted him in the mouth. He was not belted.

Bucky was in a quandary. He couldn't unload horses without a ramp. If a horse leaped from a high boxcar to the right-of-way he might break one foreleg or both. Horses were not Arizona jackrabbits.

Happily there was a loading chute down the track. Rough Riders ripped the heavy gates and floors from it and made ramps. Now all they had to find was pasture and water for the horses now standing dejectedly along the right-of-way.

A nearby farm had plenty of standing grass and a watertank beside a windmill. Bucky asked the farmer if he'd allow the horses to water and then graze a short time on the farmer's pasture. The farmer told him he'd have to pay two bucks a head.

"Haven't you any patriotism?" Bucky demanded. "These are Rough Riders' horses. They're going to Cuba to fight for your freedom."

"You don't mean my freedom," the old man returned. "You're going to take Cuba and some other islands away from a weak nation so the United States millionaires in sugar and hemp can rob the natives instead of them being robbed by Spain."

Bucky said, "We'll pay the two bucks a head."

The orders from Roosevelt were to spend the night at this siding. Rough Riders slept on the ground, mosquitoes banqueting. Next morning they chewed hardtack washed down with well water and loaded their horses — and then sat eight hours in the boiling sun waiting for the trail crew to holler *all aboard.*

"Why don't we move?" Bucky asked the conductor, who shrugged.

"Ain't got no orders to move," the conductor said.

"Before we get out of here the horses will need to be watered and pastured again," Bucky said.

The conductor said, "Blame it on the war," and walked away.

Finally the train began to move. The conductor hopped into Bucky's car. Tampa, Florida, was the next stop, two days away.

"Two days?" Bucky echoed. "No rest or hay stop for horses?"

"That's our orders. Straight through. Two days, cowboy."

Two days passed without horsefeed or water . . . and still no Tampa. Finally a rest stop was made. Gaunt horses drank gallons of water and ate harsh reed hay they'd have disdained eating in Arizona.

Finally at dawn on the fifth day the train ground to a slow halt. Bucky cocked his head and wondered what that somewhat familiar sound was. He'd not heard it for years. Then it occurred to him he was hearing the ocean.

"That's the sound of breakers," he told another Arizonian. "I remember it from Virginia. Kind of a soothing sound, isn't it, though?"

"The sound of the wind in a spruce on an Arizonian mountain would sound a hell of a lot better to me," the cowboy said in disgust. "Wonder how many days we'll spend in this saltgrass place?"

"War'll be over before we fire a shot," another cowboy said.

The first cowboy said, "That'll be good. This isn't what the books say. If they didn't shoot a deserter this cowboy'd go over the hill."

Bucky grinned but he, too, was sick and tired of red tape and Washington's delays. He asked the conductor where they were.

"Nine miles north of Tampa."

"How long we going to be here?" Bucky asked.

Again the conductor shrugged. "God knows, I'd guess — but I don't reckon God gives a goddamn. They tell me the

Tampa yards are full of cars to here and gone, the reason this train didn't pull in."

"Here comes somebody on hossback," a private said.

The courier had come to tell Captain O'Neill the Rough Riders had established a camp a mile ahead. "Water and hay there," he said.

The heat was intense. The humidity was very high. Soon man and horse were wringing wet.

The camp consisted of dirty tents with rope corrals. Hay was baled swampgrass with little — if any — nourishment.

Here Company A loitered for five long, torrid days before news came that if the Rough Riders jammed their way into Tampa there might be an outside chance of boarding a troop ship.

By that time most of the Rough Riders would have returned home, had they been able. As a war the Spanish-American War was a complete walkaway for Uncle Sam.

From all indications at the rate Uncle Sam was winning the war should soon be over.

"But you got to leave your horses

behind," the courier said. "No room on board for horses!"

"What?" Bucky demanded, wondering if he heard correctly.

"No horses. Commandante Roosevelt orders you to board *without* horses!"

Bucky's face fell. What was a cavalry charge without mounted men? But this was war. An order was an order.

Grumbling ran through Company A when the order came to desert their mounts. Bucky knew that some of his cowboys would have gladly deserted had they had the chance and could they have successfully escaped.

He himself might have even gone with them in such an event. He was sick and tired of this so-called war. What had started in high hopes was ending in the muddy muck of Florida's torrid climate.

"How do we get to Tampa," Captain William Owen O'Neill asked scornfully. "We supposed to maybe leg it?"

"Your humor is not fitting to the occasion," the college-graduate courier stated flatly. "A troop train will back in soon. You are to board it. Are my orders clear, Captain O'Neill?"

"Very clear, sir," Bucky cynically stated.

Arizona's Rough Riders waited six hours. No troop train arrived. A coal train did back up though, and the Rough Riders climbed onto its dirty cars, sure that the coal would be delivered at the dock to be used on a troop carrier.

They were correct. A half hour later they piled out of the coal cars, black with soot and dirty and filthy.

Tampa boiled with war fever. Everywhere were men in uniform. They stared at the Rough Riders for some looked like black-faced entertainers. White teeth glistened in ebony faces.

Word seeped down that there might be room for the Rough Riders on the *Yucatan*. Carrying their rifles, the Arizonians swarmed out on the dock.

One gray troop carrier, loaded with soldiers, was leaving the dock, its band playing *Old Glory*. The *Yucatan* slid next into dock.

"Here goes," Bucky said, and leaped on board, for the troop ship fairly brushed the dock.

"Who are you?" a uniformed

figure demanded.

"Captain Bucky O'Neill, commander of the Arizona unit of the Rough Riders. Come up the gangplank, men, and make it snappy."

"But Captain O'Neill —"

"But *nothing,*" Bucky snapped. "Climb aboard, boys!"

"But New Mexicans are supposed to board, not Arizonians."

"Goodby New Mexico," Bucky said, waving at the waiting New Mexicans on the dock. Then to his men, "Break up and scatter and they'll never find us to kick us off."

When the *Yucatan* slid away from the dock all of Arizona Company A were safely aboard, the New Mexicans having been forced to stay behind. Bucky and his cowboys waved at the New Mexicans who didn't wave back.

"What a hell of a war," a private said.

Bucky silently agreed. He'd seen not a trace of his commander, Theodore Roosevelt, the lion hunter. Rough Riders were now infantry men, sans horses. It hadn't turned out the way he'd expected.

He spat sourly into the Gulf of Mexico.

CHAPTER 15

Prescott housewives had sewed an Arizona Territory flag for the Rough Riders. This was hung from a rifle tied to the ship's rail.

Other troopships were strung out ahead and behind the *Yucatan*. Within a few minutes a private said shakily, "Somethin' I et don't agree with me. The sky is down where the sea should be."

He leaned far out and emptied. Bucky said, "You're seasick, Joe. When I lived in Virginia I went sailing a lot and —" He couldn't finish his sentence. He too leaned far out and lost his breakfast.

"Cripes, I miss my horse," a cowboy from Fredonia said.

The Rough Riders slept that night on deck. Next morning the hot sun shimmered on dancing whitecaps. Seasick men hung to rails. Bucky's seasickness happily had passed.

"We've sailed all day," a private said, "an' my map says it's about eighty miles from the tip of Florida to Cuba."

"We're circling the island's east tip," Bucky informed. "Action is around Santiago, I understand."

"Where's this Santiago?"

"In the middle of Cuba, about — but on the south side," Bucky informed, then added, "but maybe what I heard isn't true, Jake."

Bucky had heard that Uncle Sam's fleet had the Spanish fleet bottled up in Santiago Harbor defying the Spanish to come out and fight. Beyond Santiago to the north was a hill called *El Cerro de San Juan* — San Juan Hill — where Spanish troops had dug in and were bombarding the United States fleet at long range, but apparently inflicting little, if any, damage.

The *Yucatan* rode sea-anchor for days beyond the range of San Juan's batteries while the American leadership planned strategy.

"Why sit here?" a Rough Rider said. "Let's take the damn hill and be done with it!''

"Where's Teddy?" somebody asked.

Finally the Rough Riders sans horses were landed uneventfully on a sandy beach covered with sand crabs and green moss. Mosquitoes buzzed by the millions, many carrying malaria.

Landing was made without firing a shot. Rough Riders pitched camp and began fighting gnats, flies and mosquitoes.

All was confusion and sweat and scalding tropical heat. Tom Horn and his mules had made it although the mounts of the Rough Riders had not. "Mebbe Roosevelt expects us to ride the damn' mules to battle," an Arizona cowboy grumbled.

"With or without sitting on the packs?" another Arizonian sourly asked. "What a hell of a cavalry man I am, on foot in this damn hot, stinkin' Cuba!"

Tom's mules had just been heaved overboard to swim to shore. One mule evidently had his compass bearings set wrong for he swam out to sea, a thing that made both Bucky and Tom grin.

"I guess he didn't want no part of this phony war," Tom Horn said. "Reckon he'd be in South America by now?"

"He'd hit Jamaica before he'd hit South America," Bucky said.

"I never was no hand at geography in school," Tom Horn said. "What's the biggest town in Jamaica?"

"I studied the map just before I left home," Bucky said, "so I know Kingston is Jamaica's biggest town. You reckon the mule's pulling a dray in Kingston?"

"The way he was swimmin' so fast when I last saw him I think he was in such a hurry he'd swim clean past an island," Tom Horn said.

Tom and Bucky caught the mules as they came clambering ashore with water dripping from them. Each mule had a halter that had a rather long rope tied to it and therefore the mules were easy to catch.

The rope hadn't interfered with their swimming, either. The mules were angry and wanted to bite and kick but a lash with the free end of their halter ropes soon took that out of them.

The beach looked like a huge anthill. Companies were gathering in groups, and other men were catching mules as they swam ashore. Tom told Bucky about running face to face with Colonel Leonard Wood, with whom Tom had served on the Apache frontier.

"Twelve years since I last saw him, Bucky, and the ol' boy sure has got fat. He'll steam up when he starts climbin' San Juan Hill, you can bet on that."

Bucky grinned. "You won't find him climbing San Juan. Fat officers such as he is die in bed, Tom."

"And not from bullet wounds," an Arizonian stated.

Tom Horn spoke to Bucky. "This should give you material for a lot of stories. I read one of yours in *Cosmopolitan* when up in Wyoming. You swing a wicked but true pen, friend."

"Thanks, Tom." Bucky grinned and batted at a thousand or so hovering mosquitoes. "Yeah, this is background for a story or two, but what a heck of a way to get it, huh?"

Scouts returned sweaty and thirsty. Next morning Rough Riders moved into the steaming jungle.

"We're some Rough Riders," a man from Thatcher said. "God, what I wouldn't give for a horse!''

"This ain't like Teddy said it'd be,''
another Arizonian said.

Last night's rain had made guinea grass
slippery. Flametrees were scarlet in flower.
Squawking parrots flew from *mimosa*
trees. Slimy snakes slipped through wet
reeds into swamps.

That noon they camped on a flat area
in the high *gumabra* grass. Suddenly a
rainstorm came from nowhere. Lightning
smashed the sky. Thunder bellowed. Then
the rain ceased.

That night they pitched camp in another
clearing. Guards were posted. Men tried to
sleep on cold damp reeds, most of them
already sick with dysentery, all of them
lonesome for Arizona's grand deserts and
lofty snowcapped mountains.

"Why would any U. S. millionaire want
this damn country?'' a man grumbled.

Another laughed. "Millions in
sugarcane, buddy. They want it so Spain
can't have it.''

"So that's why we're here in this muck
and slime with a billion mosquitoes,
huh?''

"That's the way I figure it.''

"Where's Teddy?" somebody asked. "He was going to lead us, remember?"

"He's out on a cruiser way beyond the range of fire watching through field glasses, they say."

Rough Riders were circling wide to approach San Juan Hill from the north for the Hill's batteries were trained south onto where the American fleet had bottled up the Spanish fleet in Santiago bay.

When morning came rumor said they'd engage the enemy. Bucky's throat was dry. His heart thudded. He remembered making his grandiose farewell speech in the Prescott plaza.

He'd said that with Arizona men fighting the enemy Arizona would thus gain statehood more rapidly. "Who would not die for a star in the flag?" he'd dramatically finished.

San Juan Hill was ahead, now. Bucky saw men die and not for stars in a flag, either. For the first time he realized the hell of warfare.

The element was simple. You killed or got killed. You killed a man who didn't hate you and whom you didn't hate. But you had to kill him before he killed you.

Spaniards shot German Mausers. This Mauser was perhaps the best rifle in warfare at that time. Packed with smokeless powder, each firing of a Mauser left no telltale smoke-trail, as did the old American rifles.

Each time a Rough Rider shot a revealing plume of blue smoke went upward to mark his position for the Spanish sharpshooters who had the upper hand, being at a higher altitude and shooting down.

On Bucky's left a friend from Seligman slipped forward on his face. Bucky thought at first the man had merely slipped and fell but the friend didn't get up nor did he move.

Bucky then realized the man had been shot. He felt shaken and wished he'd not made such a high-faluting farewell speech.

General Young's Regulars took the right flank with Rough Rider Troop L to the left. Bucky's command, Rough Rider Troop A, took the center position. The date was July 1, 1898.

Within twenty minutes, Americans had taken the base of San Juan hill, a brush-covered upthrust. Here Rough Riders had a twenty minute respite.

Captain McClintock had been seriously wounded and had been carried via stretcher behind lines. Major Bodie of Company A also had suffered bullet wounds.

This left Bucky O'Neill in complete command of Company A. A sweaty runner came in with a message from Captain Howze of the Regulars. Had Bucky located the Spanish snipers?

Indeed, Bucky had located the deadly snipers, the ones who'd been taking the biggest toll of American troops. The Spanish sharpshooters were holed up along the top ridge of rocky San Juan Hill and, in Bucky's estimation, the only way to route them was to storm up San Juan hill.

"You intend to storm the Hill, then, Captain O'Neill? Shall I impart this knowledge to Captain Howze?"

"You have my permission. Tell Captain Howze that inside of ten minutes Company A will begin its climb. If we don't silence those snipers they'll lie there and kill every one of us."

The runner disappeared into the brush.

Bucky breathed deeply and hoped he'd made the right tactical decision. He looked at his watch and let ten minutes elapse, his men hidden as best as possible in the brush with Spanish rifle fire occasionally breaking out in savage bursts.

"Time's up, men. Ready?"

"As ready as we'll ever be, Bucky."

"Check rifles and ammunition. Ready, men? Up the goddamned Hill we go!"

Spanish rifle fire was murderous. Rough Riders faltered, stopped, fell; still, the Arizonians pushed on.

High on San Juan Hill a hidden Spanish sniper laid his swarthy cheek against the sleek smooth stock of his new German-made Mauser. Slowly, carefully, he took accurate aim at one of the approaching Rough Riders.

He didn't know the name of the man on whom he centered his rifle's sights. The blue-eyed man below didn't know the name of the brown-eyed Spaniard.

The blue-eyed man didn't hate the brown-eyed man. The brown-eyed man didn't hate the man with light blue eyes.

But this was war and you killed or you got killed. And the brown-eyed man slowly squeezed his trigger, the Mauser recoiling sharply against his stocky shoulder.

The bullet hit the blue-eyed man in the throat. It broke his neck and dropped him dead in his tracks.

A Rough Rider screamed, "My God, they've killed Bucky!"

The rest is history. Arizona's Rough Riders finally took San Juan Hill, leaving not a Spanish sniper alive. With San Juan's batteries silenced United States warships moved into Santiago Harbor and annihilated the Spanish fleet within a few hours. William Owen O'Neill was buried with full military honors in the cemetery at the base of San Juan Hill. With him to his grave went quite a few of his Arizona companions, good and true men.

The coming April his body was removed to Arlington National Cemetery where he lies today beside his soldier father, Captain John O'Neill. At long last Virginia's quail hunter had returned home.

Arizona mourned in pride. Two hundred Arizonians — neighbors and friends and admirers of Bucky —

journeyed to Arlington National Cemetery to attend Bucky's second funeral.

After Bucky's death saddle-tough Arizonians smashed up San Juan Hill to silence the batteries and the snipers. They took the Hill in bloody fighting, some hand to hand, and they lost men — but they took it, just as Americans later took Iwo Jima and other supposedly impregnable fortresses.

With the batteries on San Juan Hill silenced United States warships moved ponderously into Santiago Harbor to annihilate the Spanish fleet on July 3. The Spanish-American War lasted only one hundred and thirteen days.

All in all twenty-eight hundred and three men and a hundred and thirteen officers were killed in the war. Many others, though, died of dysentery and fever and malaria and other tropical diseases.

Today in the plaza of Bucky O'Neill's home town of Prescott, Arizona, is a bronze statue of a Rough Rider mounted on a wild Arizona cowpony.

The Rough Rider leans forward in saddle, the endless Arizona wind whipping back his flat-brimmed hat. That statue was cast by the great Solon Borglum, brother of Gutzon Borglum who sculpted the enormous Mount Rushmore National Memorial — the four faces of four United States presidents — in the tough granite of South Dakota's Black Hills.

That Rough Rider is a replica of Bucky O'Neill.

The epitaph on Bucky O'Neill's gravestone reads:

William O. O'Neill
Mayor of Prescott, Arizona
Captain Troop A, First U. S.
Volunteer Cavalry, Rough Riders
Brevet Major
Born Feb. 2, 1860
Killed July 1, 1898
At San Juan Hill, Cuba
"Who would not die for a new star
in the Flag?"